For God Loves
Foolish People

Satbir Chadha

Vitasta
Let Knowledge Spread

Published by
Renu Kaul Verma
Vitasta Publishing Pvt Ltd
2/15, Ansari Road, Daryaganj,
New Delhi - 110 002
info@vitastapublishing.com

ISBN: 978-93-82711-09-4
© **Satbir Chadha,** 2014

Typeset by Vitasta Publishing Pvt Ltd
Photography and Cover Design by Amlan Dutta
Print: Repro India Limited, Mumbai

To

My husband Balbir

for that shared glass of beer

in Bangalore

Acknowledgement

My son Sarabjit saw my talent for writing and encouraged me. My friend Kiran Babel pushed me to publish and guided me in sending articles to the *Hindustan Times*. Manorama Jaffa of AWIC threw me a challenge saying that if I was not publishing then I was only writing diaries.

I am grateful to Renu Kaul Verma of Vitasta Publishing for publishing my book and to Veena Batra for her very competent editing.

Preface

The book describes an idyllic childhood spent in the small town of Haldwani, in the foothills of Nainital, in the beginning of the nineteen fifties, where nature played a symphony and the lives of the simple people kept tune with it. It is a peep into the times; with the author travelling to Dehradun, where her maternal grandparents live, to pristine Bombay where her father is starting a new business, to and fro with the circumstances. The narrative includes the life and culture of the sturdy '*Bhotia*' tribe that lives in the snow-covered mountains. While building the character of '*Bauji*' her grandfather, who had the most influence on her, the other characters are brought in, the mother and father, grandmother, the grandfather's sister, uncles and aunts and all cousins and friends.

Important also are the different animals, birds, reptiles, and even insects, and how by observing these, many lessons of life were learnt, especially snakes, who made exciting encounters, but were hugely feared. All episodes about them are real and experienced by the author.

As the narrative proceeds with childhood experiences, the history of the cultures of Punjabis, of Sikhs, of the political scene, the building of the 'Gurudwara' in Haldwani, are interestingly intertwined with the story. There is the grandfather's elder brother remarrying when his wife dies, but not allowing his sister to marry when she becomes a widow, even though she asserts her right to do so, and even though it was the accepted practice in Punjab. Instead he exiles his own wife to Punjab while he lives in Kathgodam, exposing the vanity and insensitivity of men.

The rituals and wedding ceremonies are a peep into that culture, when people had pure fun. The train journey to Dehradun reads like a romantic fantasy. Included also is the narration of how the complete demography and ecology of the area between Nainital and Rampur, a region two to three hundred square miles, changed with the history of India, when along with Independence came the partition of the country. The tantrums of the governments of the time, having the whole government staff and documents being shifted to hill-stations in the summer, must be having no parallel anywhere else.

The part of childhood spent in Bombay is a total contrast, seeing the visiting dignitaries like Queen Elizabeth and President Kennedy, and even meeting Mother Teresa. College in Bombay is an enlightening experience, with this particular batch pioneering the SUPW programme, which has since been integrated in all educational institutions—adopting a village of 'Waarli Tribes', and working with them to help uplift their standard of living.

Such a pampered childhood, such learned parents and grandparents, doting on the author's every whim, suddenly comes to nought when they think nothing of her wishes, ambitions, choices, capabilities, fantasies, and nip her feelings the way a gardener nips an overgrown hedge with a pair of garden scissors, because it suits their social status to get her married into a wealthy and popular family. For the first time she comes face to face with hypocrisy, and its permanent existence! Almost as in a child marriage, a delightful and carefree girl is simply delivered to an unknown family, to struggle and learn how to be a 'housewife'.

The heartbroken young girl can only choke on her sobs; she is rendered so helpless.

The love of nature, frequent trips to Haldwani and Nainital, and books, her major crutch in life soon enable her to rise above this adversity, and find a new purpose in life. In helping her father-in-law, who had made his fortune in war battered Assam, she finds a new confidence, and learns from him to take problems head-on, and not ponder on petty issues. Making an important place for herself in the new family, gradually earning the respect of the elders and love of the children, she emphasizes the value of a good education.

With four grown-up sons and five grandchildren, she finally decides to get a Laptop, and become a writer. The writer wants to show that what happened a century earlier, and what will happen a century later, are linked with a fine thread, while describing an enviable childhood.

Finally, there is Daddy, who, suffering the scorn of his father whom he adores, pines silently for his wife, spending the last years of his life suffering from alcoholism and hydrocephalus— a brilliant man, doddering and crumbling, sadly.

Chapter 1

The School Horse

I was born and brought up in Nainital, the best hill station I know. All the houses there are on the slopes of the hills, and the hills surround the large lake on all sides. The lake always remains green, reflecting the hills, while the clear blue sky keeps changing, occasionally grey with clouds; sometimes greyer with darker clouds; and full of stars in the night—when the lake reflects the lights of the town in its deep blue waters! As a child, I was constantly with my grandfather, who was very influential, powerful and wealthy. Being his first and favourite grandchild, I had unlimited access to anything I asked for—nobody could hazard me a denial.

The law in Nainital then did not allow motor cars to enter the town, to maintain the pristine beauty of the place, and everybody followed the law. So we all walked to wherever we had to go or hired a horse. The old and sick people were carried in a 'Dandee' by four coolies. Now, I had been on a trip to Bombay to be with Daddy for some time, as he had started a new business there and was living in a small house. I had seen the children there going to school in a 'school-bus', so I began to pester my grandfather, whom we all called 'Bauji', "Bauji, I don't want to walk to school. I get very tired and even Kamli (my ayah) starts panting while climbing up the hill."

"But Gugan, we all have to walk, there is no other way in Nainital," Bauji said. Gugan is what I was called lovingly by everyone when I was a child.

"Bauji, you are so big, you can do whatever you want. When you go to the Latt Sahib's (the Governor's) house, you take the car. Even the Latt Sahib goes in the car with his children. Why can't I go to school in the car?"

"Bacchoo," said my grandfather, "when the Latt Sahib comes to the market, he comes on his horse. If we drive cars in Nainital, the whole town will become dirty with the smoke of the petrol. Besides, it is so healthy to walk; you can digest all the food that you eat, fast, and you can eat more mangoes when you come back!"

"Then I will also go to school on a horse, like the Latt Sahib," I said. Instinctively, I knew when my case was won. "If I go to school tomorrow, it will be on a horse, or I will stay at home!"

Thereafter Bauji spoke to a horse-man, and he was to come every morning at nine to take me to school, which was on another hill across from my house. I was so excited that I jumped on the horseback, while Bauji's instructions went on and on. "Hold the reins tight, don't let the horse go near the edge, let him eat the grass only on the hillside near the school building, don't stop to pluck flowers," and so on! I trotted off to school, waving at other children on the way, too happy to bother about their envy.

After some days though, the novelty and enthusiasm wore off, and the trip began to get boring. Narain, the horse-man, was too strict with me, "You can't do this or Bauji will be angry with me; you can't do that or Bauji will be angry with me." I could not even shout out the name of a friend passing by, for, "the horse may get scared and jump, and then Bauji will be angry with me." Ugh! my childhood ego would not let me admit it, but I began to crave my walk to school—it was so much more fun. Anyway, towards the end of the month I had decided to tell Bauji to stop Narain and 'Tojo' the horse from coming, when Narain fell ill, and his son Jeet Singh came to take me to school.

Now Jeet Singh, or 'Jitwa' as we called him, was very young, barely out of his teens, slim and of medium height, a fair complexion and handsome 'Pahari' features.

As soon as we set out from home, he teased me, "Now

I know why Tojo was becoming thin; he has to carry a plump little lady every day."

Though fat was considered healthy back then, I still lashed back, "Oh you keep quiet! Your father's not been feeding his horse well, and you are blaming me. Wait till I tell Bauji about this."

"Bauji? Don't tell him, I was only joking!"

"Aha! So you're scared of Bauji, I know."

"Scared? What scared? I'm not scared of anyone, not even my own father."

"Then what?"

"I was thinking, why bother Bauji, he has so many more important things to take care of."

"Hmm.Do you know the way to school?"

"Yes, father told me. So let's go, so you don't get late."

Jitwa was cautious but relaxed, and invariably we chatted a lot. I would ask him about his home. He told me that he lived with his father. His mother was no more and his sister had been married off. This made me sad, for I had never seen anyone who didn't have a mother, though in Haldwani I had seen children with two mothers! I would ask him every day, "How did your mother die?" He said, "I was very small, and I was told that she had fallen sick." Then I wanted to know, "Why did she fall sick? Why did the doctor not give her good medicine, and why did he not make her alright?" After a week he got fed up and told me, "If you talk about my mother, I will not come from tomorrow." I thought of the boring trips with Narain, and said, "Ok, I will not talk of your mother."

I asked him about his school, and he said that he had gone to school for a couple of years and then stopped. I asked him why, and he said," I hate school, I hate teachers, I hate to read and write. I'll never go to school."

"But you have to go to school," I said.

"No way! No one can ever force me to go to school," he said.

I marvelled at his guts—we kids could never imagine not going to school, like it or hate it, but Jitwa here was so bold, so strong, that he could not be forced to go to school. Wow! I began to admire his confidence.

And he enthralled me with details of his life, which were routine for him, but extraordinary for me. Feeding grass to the horse, rubbing his back, walking him; feeding, walking, and milking his cow; and his chickens, some forty or fifty of them—enough to get them some extra cash from selling the eggs; all this was a delightful experience in my view! Therefore, nearly a month later, I declared to him that I wanted to marry him!

He got such a start that he sat down on the road, held his head in his hands and laughed. He laughed till his body rocked with laughter. I became serious and said, "Jitwa, are you feeling worried because I am small?" But he said, "Why are you saying such foolish things?"

I was hurt. I said, "I am not foolish. I have to become a Dulhan when I get a little older, so I have decided to become your Dulhan. First of all, you have no mother, so I'll take care of you and your father. Also you have a horse and a cow and chicks. Besides, I will look pretty sitting outside a hut on the lonely hillside, like the painting on the wall in Sahji's library."

"Oh, is that why you'll get married?" he said, and laughed more. I became red with anger! Totally disgusted, I did not speak again on the way, and in the evening when we reached home, I was thrilled to see that Daddy had come over from Bombay. In that excitement, I forgot all about Jitwa.

But Daddy noticed him and asked about him, and told him to sit in the veranda, while he pampered me with books and other gifts he had brought from Bombay. I became busy with the new game of Ludo Daddy had brought and the new books.

Meanwhile Daddy asked all about Jitwa. He could not bear to see such a smart young man wasting his life without education or a career. He spoke to him at length and encouraged him to try for a better career. By late evening, they had decided that Jitwa would join the army and for a couple of months Dad would arrange a teacher to teach him to read and write, at least enough to pass the army test.

Anyway, next morning, I announced to Bauji that I wanted to walk to school again. I was sincerely missing my friends and how we used to walk together, singing and joking and chatting all the way; admiring new flowers on the hillside, and chasing the butterflies in the morning sun. Sometimes we'd be up to mischief, and coax unsuspecting tourists to touch the innocent looking plant, Bichhoo Buti, and see them burn from itching; then we'd show them how rubbing the leaves of another plant would make the itching vanish magically!

This time when Dad returned to Bombay, Mom and I went with him. I joined school there, and thus began my big-city life, that has never ended.

A year later we came back to Nainital for a vacation. Things were very bad in our country. China had started a war with India, attacking our North-Eastern borders. We had very few soldiers on the border, and they lacked proper equipment and gear. All the money was going into the war. Everywhere there were pictures of a sad Prime Minister, our dear Jawaharlal Nehru, who had trusted the Chinese, and they had betrayed him. In Bombay, my mother had to buy sugar at Rs. seven a kilo, and from the ration shop we got reddish wheat. The 'chapattis' of its flour were dry and hard. All the women were knitting socks for the soldiers. For the first time, I heard words like, 'costly' and 'afford', and saw Daddy feeling very upset. He decided that we go to Nainital for some months, so he could struggle with the business alone.

Some days later, a very young pahari girl came to meet Bauji. She must have been fifteen or sixteen, was of short height and very pretty, but also confused and very sad. Bauji made some phone calls and sent her with the manager to a government office. In the evening they returned carrying a big tin trunk between them, the kind we used to carry on a long train journey. They set it down in the veranda, and the girl sat down and began to weep. We gave her water and tried to comfort her, when Bauji came out. She rose and touched his feet, and took out from inside her shawl, a large rolled photograph she was carrying. Bauji nodded sympathetically, and I looked curiously at the photo. The man in the photograph had a robust and cheerful face with long moustaches, that looked somewhat familiar. I stared, trying to recollect, when I saw the name at the bottom, 'Sepoy Jeet Singh. Kumaon Regiment. Killed In Action.'

My heart missed a beat, and cried for the young girl, whom he had married just a month before the war. I was very sad, and suddenly felt very grown-up.

☺☺☹

Chapter 2

The Beginning Of The Story

As a child the sight that thrilled me the most was the sight of mango blossoms. The day the first mango blossoms appeared on our mango trees, it was the best news we could share, my grandfather and I. Every time I stepped out of the house, I turned my head to look up at them. The next few weeks went by observing how much each tree had blossomed, and which blossoms were the healthiest. Each mango tree held a story for *Bauji*; about where he had acquired the sapling, which year, and which tree had been specially grafted with two different varieties to give an amazing new flavour and sweetness. My grandfather was a highly learned and powerful man in Haldwani. He was the Municipal Commissioner there for eighteen years. Brought up in a feudal society, he lived like a tough patriarch, and most people looked up to him. He was philanthropic by nature, and had access to resources with which he could help them; like money, and influence over the right people in government. Very few people denied him a request, or an order. I loved watching when he prepared an order to be passed in the Council, then folded it and put it in an envelope, then melted the red Government seal with a candle to seal the envelope with his Commissioner's stamp. It felt so important. But to most people he was a man to be feared as that was the personality he had created over the years. If *Bauji* was sitting at his shop, no ladies would pass that way, fearing his scorn, for he believed women had no business to be walking alone on the roads, even though they were in '*Purda*'. He was autocratic with most men too; his eyes could pierce through a man's soul, so no one dared to tell him a lie. But women he respected, and felt very protective towards them. It was well-known that I was his only weakness. I never actually saw him at it, but everyone knew that he knocked off a bottle of scotch every night, with nearly a kilo of mutton or chicken curry! I was only happy that he shared my love for mangoes.

In the summer months in Haldwani, a small town in the foothills of Nainital, we get cyclonic rain or dust storms very often, and after each such storm, I would rush out to assess the damage to my blossoms. Invariably also, a large number of parrots would descend upon our garden. So we'd put some noisy contraptions on the trees to shoo away the birds. These were large empty tins, tied with a long rope to the tree. When the rope was pulled, they banged against the branches of the tree to create a racket, and the birds would fly away, and we'd protect the precious blossoms! Actually, I was patiently waiting for the blossoms to fall and be replaced by tiny green mangoes. And then I'd wait for them to grow into big, plump, yellow ripe mangoes. The taste of the ripe mangoes, especially the ones that grew in our garden was truly divine!

Today in our old house, all the trees are gone except two, my favourite two. The garden has been replaced by small and big houses; it is now a colony. I stroll through the colony, and stop at every step, remembering each tree as it was; here a peach tree, here a grapefruit one, whose fruit almost always went waste as few people had a taste for grapefruit, and fewer knew of its nutritional value; here was a 'Pahari Kela', that gave us huge bananas, the only ones I have ever eaten with seeds, the pulp thicker and sweeter than any other. I go to the place where the water pond was—some lotus would grow in it, but it was also full of toads, and in winter, small though it was, it got its share of ducks basking in the sun! When I stop, people wonder what I'm looking for—they don't know that I'm looking at my past!

As I walk further, I pass by the place where a tiny steam engine used to be kept. I was told that it was a leftover from the time when my grandfather had constructed the Kathgodam Railway Station, the very first railhead there. It had no engine or machinery, only its empty rusty body, and its lovely big wheels, digging into the soft ground. But what a thrill it gave us children to play on it! One of us would sit on its rickety seat and be the engine driver, while others played the role of coal-fenders, some played travellers and some played coolies, and in command was the 'Guard' with the red and green flags, and all the attendant importance! A rusty old relic helped to create a whole travelling experience for us small children all those years.

There were also lots of bricks, wooden logs and other construction material lying around. We didn't need much creativity to start building our mini houses, brick by brick, and when they were about three feet high, we were more than satisfied—we had built a big house!

Somewhere there'd be a veranda also, for in those days, kitchens used to be outside the house. Bathrooms were there only in our house—no one else had that luxury—people simply walked to the jungle, which started just outside our garden wall and extended up to the high hills, to relieve themselves. But when the houses were built the fights would start. 'A' would want 'B' in her house, but 'B' said, no way, she'd rather live with 'C', who said, "I want no nonsense, I'm breaking my house, and I'll make a new one tomorrow, where I'll live with 'D'." So much construction activity went on in that part of the garden!

The next patch of ground after this had nothing much growing on it even then, and it's pretty much the same now. I cross it. And then there is a row of small houses, all of different shapes, but all having big courtyards and verandas. These houses bring so much warmth to my heart. There was a kind lady, Mrs Tiku, who out of concern for me, because I had been sent to all the schools in Haldwani and had refused to join any, accepted my grandfather's offer to start a new school, one that I would like. She lived in one half of our house, her husband was the manager of a large fruit preserving factory. She was highly educated. She started the school in two spare rooms with her daughter Vinita and me as her first two students. She had three more children. Ashok, the eldest, was much older to us, Vinita a couple of years older than me, Asha much younger, and Arun, who was my age. All of us kids were very friendly, and were together all the time for we shared the same large veranda and lawns.

Within a year, she had so many students that our family had to let her have two more houses to expand her classes.

Now, imagine a school in the middle of a fruit orchard! We kids climbed trees in the lunch break, and played hop-scotch in the verandas of those houses, using smooth white pebbles picked from the cobbled pathway of our house.

Mrs Tiku changed forever the education system in Haldwani. Now we had proper note books instead of wooden slates, chairs and desks, smart and dedicated teachers, a playground, which was our own green lawn, and even 'bicycle rickshaws' to ferry children. She instilled the importance of English language, which was earlier taught only after the eighth standard. All the schools started after hers have followed her pattern. The first time we celebrated Independence Day in school, it was the talk of the town; all the students wore white clothes, and when the patriotic songs were sung, along with the National Anthem, we had lumps in our throats, and some teachers actually wept. The euphoria of a free nation was still fresh in every mind and we children had been told so many tales of patriots and freedom fighters, that we almost felt we knew them personally. Even Bauji congratulated Mrs Tiku on the event.

After these school blocks was the house that had been built the earliest. The one we lived in was built later and very elaborately. This old house had a huge tamarind tree in the courtyard, My grandfather had taken the advice of old and experienced farmers, who had calculated the age of this tree to be more than a hundred years old. So it was decided to let it remain as it was, and a concrete platform was built around it, on which we sat and chatted and which would prevent the tree from falling on the house in case of a storm, or if the tree weakened. I walked to this place now, remembering the majesty of this tree—it's branches spread over three adjoining houses, and all we kids had to do was to climb to the roof of any of them and enjoy its juicy and tangy fruit—even carry some home for Mom. The tree was so well endowed that it never disappointed us; there was always enough fruit for everyone! As I grew up I learnt that on each flowering, this tree would give up to 150-200 kg of fruit per crop. I still find it amazing. As I am walking to the spot to pay homage to the old tree, I'm stared at curiously by people who live in that house now. Their courtyard is now flat and tiled, my tamarind tree having fallen to a massive cyclonic storm when I was 11 years old. The concrete boundary, the concrete floor around it, and some earth too was uprooted as it fell on the roof of that very house it had shaded for years, but thankfully no one had been hurt. That day we had stood around the tree in solemn tribute, with heavy hearts, sad, as if we had lost a loved one.

I went walking up the boulevard outside our house, the same sliver of peace with a rain water stream gushing down its middle, and I got a great feeling when I saw that the school that was started for my benefit is still doing well and expanding. They now have new buildings, lawns, gardens, and bright new little faces every year. I feel good that, though it was not my doing, I became a catalyst in the creation of this institution, "Tiku's Modern School.". Mrs Tiku is no more, but the third generation of the family is running the school very well. Compared to other schools in Haldwani, it is better maintained and has a big lawn with beautiful trees!

Close to where this school is now is the place where the

'Bhotia' tribe used to come down from the snowing upper hills and settle here for the three to four winter months. The Bhotia's are a shepherd tribe who live at very high altitudes in the Kumaon hills. They also keep shepherd dogs called Bhotia dogs, which have furry black skin and are known to be very silent, but very ferocious. The Bhotias would come down every winter and pitch their tents from Tehri Pulia to where Tiku's school is now. They spoke their own language and I was fascinated by the mono-syllabic long hoots they had devised to call out to each other. They would cup their mouths with their hands, and effortlessly say "h-o-oo-o—o—oo," but the effect was such that the voice carried to long distances. Then they would wait for a minute for a similar hoot back, confirming the receipt of the call. Maybe when you call people across the hills, this is what works. Nature is the best teacher, or is it 'ancient networking'?

As kids, we would often hover around the Bhotia camps, and we learnt a lot of things about them. Their men folk would take the sheep out grazing. As the sheep grazed on verdant greens, the men would knit. Very few had knitting needles, they used dry twigs.

I marvelled at the way they plucked the longest thorn from the thorn tree, and then using another thorn, dug patiently through it to make a sewing needle. The thread they used was also created out of fallen out wool, twined tightly, or thinly rolled jute.

Their kids were really cute—chubby, healthy and handsome, and could adapt anything around them to create a new game. I marvelled at the way they plucked the longest thorn from a 'thorn tree' (these are trees on which only thorns grow),and then using another thorn gradually, patiently, dig a hole on the thicker end of the thorn, to make a sewing needle! The thread they used was also created out of fallen out wool, twined tightly, or thinly rolled jute. What fascinated me the most about the Bhotias was that they never changed their clothes—I never probed whether they ever bathed or not. They would remain in the clothes they had come down in; if a garment became threadbare, they'd simply get a new garment and wear it on top. The torn one underneath continued to give insulation, which they'd need, especially when they went back to the snowbound upper hills.

I can never forget the Bhotia children; they were extremely beautiful with red cheeks, fair skin, healthy but never obese, and reticent—always remaining within their community, around the mothers or other friends. There wasn't any work allotted to the children so they mostly spent their time playing, relaxing or singing softly.

When I look back now, I feel that's how a childhood should be! I only saw smiles on those young faces, never saw them fighting; in fact I never saw any fights among any Bhotias. Of course, disputes must be happening, for they are human too, but maybe they had a great judiciary! There were never any disputes with the locals either. They did a lot of barter trading. They had products from the hills, and these they bartered for their necessities. Curiously, buttons were in great demand among them; even old broken ones were never discarded. All their resources came mainly from nature, like wool, medicinal herbs, powder of the horns of the 'Barasingha' a large hill-deer, which is said to have tremendous medicinal and aphrodisiac properties. Nature, and their knowledge, experience, and observation of it, worked together to fulfil their needs.

This tribe had been coming here for many years, and gave this place its name, 'Bhotia Parao', or abode of the Bhotias. I don't know the real reason, but they stopped coming after 1958 or so. Maybe the plains became too populated, or the hills were not so cold anymore!

The walk from our house in "Bhotia Parao" to Kathgodam was magical. The distance was three miles or a little less than five kilometres. "Bhotia Parao" was thinly populated with orchards or farms being the norm, and as we walked towards Kathgodam, we marked our distance as we passed the different farms; on the left the brothers Vidyaratan and Dharambeer, on the right the Pandeys, and then the Daundiyals, after which was the farm of Gobind Ballabh Pant, who was the first Home Minister of Independent India, then Mr Fonseca on the left—and so on. There were long green patches on both sides, and the hills were like the boundary walls of the town. Walking up—and there are only two ways you can go in Haldwani, either up or down—I'd look at all the hills one by one, make sure each furrow was where it was, every patch of brown, and the long green ridges, the dull green of the pines; and it was very re-assuring. Kathgodam was a cluster of small houses with a tiny market, pushcarts selling veggies and fruits, and our small petrol-pump, just across the beautiful hillside Railway Station.

I loved to go to the petrol pump with Daddy or my uncle or whoever went, and sit there long hours. I'd get lots of office stationery to write or scribble on and enjoyed watching the boys selling diesel, petrol or lubricants to buses and trucks that would drive up; cars in those days were rare. The measure used was 'gallons'. My earliest memory is of petrol selling at Rs. 1.25 per gallon which is equal to about five litres! That price is etched in my memory. A trip to Kathgodam always ended with my being entertained at the railway station Waiting Room to omelette and toast, and tea, served in pure white crockery with appropriate cutlery on white table cloths.

Once my Bauji, my Mom and I were travelling from Kathgodam to Dehradun, where my maternal grandparents lived, and we had loads of luggage, including a 'suraahi', an earthen water pitcher, for we used to drink only boiled water. We reached the station and were escorted by the station-master himself to our first class coupe with four berths. He kept asking us if we needed anything and if we were comfortable. I was only eager to sit by the window for I loved the view. Before the train was to pull out, the Guard ran up to my grandfather and asked if he could start the train. He waved the green flag. Obviously, it must have been only a polite gesture but it made me feel very important.

The train went thuk-thuk-thuk-thuk-shoooooon, thuk-thuk-thuk-thuk-shoooooooon; my mother taught me to identify this rhythm with the recital of a poem, or a song, or even sing God's name, rhyming with the sound of the train. To look out and notice every bush, tree, every flower, even cattle and ponies passing by—or farmers ploughing the field or women walking gracefully carrying pots on their heads, showed me how everything was so much in harmony. Now I wish we could make it as simple to travel through this life. All we have to do is to blend ourselves, our deeds, our desires, and our efforts into harmony with everything and everyone around, for God's total creation is perpetually in harmony. Then life would be a pleasant, fruitful and spiritual journey.

In five to six hours we reached Bareilly. Bareilly was a big station and a junction, and there we had to leave our smaller gauge train and shift to a broader gauge train to Dehradun. As we settled into the new coach, turbaned waiters in white uniforms, with red belts around their waists, arrived with large trays full of food. My grandfather had sent a telegram with instructions from Kathgodam, so there they were! Soup was served. Then chicken, dal, and chapattis, with warm caramel pudding to round it off. After paying the bill, my grandfather gave the waiters a princely tip of Rs. 2, and they were overwhelmed and thankful.

Reaching Dehradun, I became involved in my Nani's house. Mom's two younger brothers were there, Moni Mamaji and Amy Mamaji, and besides, the house was full of my maternal cousins. It was great fun, as they were all older, and played grown-up games, cracked wittier jokes, and pampered me a lot, though they'd sometimes sneer at my ' big-shot of a grandfather', and I'd sulk and argue till they apologized.

My Nanaji kept two buffaloes in the backyard for a supply of fresh milk for the family, and kept a lot of poultry. What upset me was that everyone had milk at breakfast, either with corn flakes or porridge, and again at bedtime, in huge cups with lots of sugar added to it, and I was also forced to drink it though I hated milk! Even in our house in Haldwani we had buffaloes, but no one ever forced me to drink milk, and no one drank milk either. In my earliest memories, whenever I awoke in the morning, Daddy or Mataji would go to the dining table where there was always a 'samovar' full of piping hot tea. They would fill a cup, and I had tea and biscuits. Milk was often added to the brandy I was given on cold winter nights, to make it taste less bitter. Brandy was our drug of choice for most problems; when we caught a cold, we drank brandy with warm milk; if we had constipation or colic, we drank brandy in warm water or honey, and when we had a loose tummy, then it was brandy with cold water. I had heard Mataji talk about women in her village applying opium mixed in water to their breasts while suckling their infants to cure them of colic and diarrhoea; decades later when I administered medicine drops to my son when he cried with colic, and I read 'phenobarbitone' a derivative of opium, on the pack, I realized that those village women were on track. The buffaloes were milked before daybreak, and by afternoon were let loose to graze on the ample greenery around. In the evenings it fascinated me when the servant went out to get the buffaloes back from grazing. I always wondered how he recognized them from the other herds returning home. This has remained a mystery for me till today. I enjoyed myself more with the chickens, and learnt to recognize them by their colour and size, and to feed them, coo to them, and count them at night. One night the count fell short by two. I pestered the servant to find out where they were, but he wouldn't tell. Later I felt a pang when I saw the chicken curry on the dining table—so this was where they had landed up! But being a non-vegetarian, the guilt did not last long; besides there were many more in the poultry-shed.

When we had to return to Haldwani, I insisted on taking home two bright chirpy hens, plump ones whom I liked. Only my grandfather was wary, for he said the Railway laws did not allow livestock to travel in passenger trains. I told him, "I'll cover them and hide them, and even keep them quiet if someone comes to check." He argued, but gave up. A large basket was bought, one with a cover and big enough to accommodate two grown up hens on the journey. When we reached Haldwani, a proper home was created for them, a large airy shelter, and they were fed and looked after properly. I loved playing with them, but after a few days I realised that they were not cheerful at all, and I was upset that they were not laying eggs either. Some people told me I would have to get a cock; innocently I asked what a cock had to do with a hen laying an egg? Ultimately over the weekend, my grandfather walked up to Mr Fonseca's farm, and came back holding a beautiful red-tailed cock, and wonders! The hens started laying lovely pink eggs every day. They were kept aside for me to eat, and they tasted wonderful.

After two weeks or so, I was told not to eat the eggs as the hen wanted to sit on them to hatch. That again was a marvellous experience. Some eight eggs were put on a large clump of dry straw, and the hen sat covering them—even as I worried that she would crush them! But this lady sat on them patiently, night and day, for three weeks. Every day I observed that in the morning and evening, the cock would 'cuckoo' to her from outside,(for she was in a closed room), and my hen would answer from inside. It was beautiful. On day twenty-one, I returned from school, and my servant took me to the hen's shed, and shut my eyes with his hands, and when he said, "open your eyes," I was enraptured by the sight. The hen was standing, and around her were seven cute little brown chickens, chucking away. The hen was trying to feed them a grain or two with her own beak. This was nothing short of God's miracle for me! It goes without saying that I visited the chicks as often as I could and marvelled at the way they grew bigger every day. Soon the mother lost interest in feeding them and my servant said, "Now they are fit to be left on their own."

Such a simple philosophy; Do not sit over kids who have learnt to hunt for their own food and can live by themselves. The mother hen moved on with her life. Beautiful!

Next, the other hen too hatched her eggs. It was a wonder to me how my servant could tell which were baby cocks and which were baby hens. I believed he had mystic powers for I was only six years old. Anyway by the end of the year, my poultry-shed had a count of over sixty heads, and they were all beautiful. They were very intelligent too. We'd leave them to wander in the garden in the afternoon, and at dusk, just stand outside the house and call, "aa-aa-aa-aa-aa," and one by one they'd all come back to their places in the shed. Nature's own great Communication Technology!

My stock of chickens had already become the envy of some of my cousins. One of them borrowed and never returned two pairs of my chicks, and gradually built up a flourishing poultry farm over the years. People in Haldwani were becoming prosperous by now. The local aristocratic families were getting richer in free India, for they were able to work better with the new class of politicians and civil servants, unlike earlier when the British had not been so easily approachable, except for a few, like Bauji. New businesses were opening up, the government was encouraging indigenous industry, but sadly, the woods were an immediate source of income for both the government and the timber traders. Roads were being built, transport was growing, and with it the related business of vehicles and spares. People without capital were getting more jobs, and more government jobs were now available. The 'Pahari' people were generally contented and happy that the country was free, happy that the soldiers were back from the World War, and happy that more young lads were getting into the coveted Armed Forces. The Sikhs who had come in from the partitioned Pakistan, uprooted from their homes and fields, were now prospering in their new occupations, and were gradually getting over the trauma of Partition, though conversations invariably veered to those episodes.

☺☻☹

Chapter 3

Daddy Dearest!

B eing such a pampered child, I could easily have grown up to be an arrogant brat had Daddy not excercised such a grounding influence on me. He was the kindest man I have ever met in my life, most generous, hard working, humble and honest. There was more power in his compassion, more strength in his soft eyes than in *Bauji's* high-handed autocratic demeanour. His most endearing quality was his immense respect for everyone, regardless of their station in life, and quietly he made sure that I learnt to respect everyone like he did. There was this episode when I was just six years old and we had gone to Bombay for the first time. We had a custom where every household shared some food with the sweeper who came to clean the washrooms and collect the garbage. One day, Mummy was busy and asked me to give some '*chapattis*' to the woman; and I, in my foolish arrogance, dropped them into her outstretched hands obviously to avoid touching her. Daddy observed this and asked me to call her back, which I did. Then in English, so that the lady would not understand, he told me to take back the chappatis, and present them to her with respect, and to even touch her hand while doing so, so that her self-respect was intact! I did that, and to this day I have never forgotten the lesson; if ever I realize that I may be hurting someone, particularly if I wound someone's self esteem, I remind myself of that episode, and make amends like Daddy taught me to.

Most of all I am indebted to him for teaching me to read and encouraging me, to always be learning new tasks, new subjects, whenever possible. He was always saying, "Satvir, read always, there is so much to learn. And if you cannot perform a task, learn it, do not lag behind another person who can do it." He was highly learned himself, having got his M A degree from Allahabad University, and his Law degree from Lucknow in 1950. One of his law teachers had been Dr Shankar Dayal Sharma, later to become the President of India. I happened to be with Daddy once in Bombay, when we were going to the 'Tea Centre' at 'Resham Bhawan' opposite Churchgate station. Dr Sharma was coming out and when he saw Daddy he hugged him happy to see him after so long. He said, "You know, if Trilok (my Daddy) and three of my other good students were in class, it never mattered to me if anyone else came or not. For me, my class was complete. Your father is one of my best students!" Such a huge compliment, and it made me so proud.

Daddy's outstanding quality was that he made friends easily, and created lasting relationships, keeping contact with his friends wherever they may be around the globe. During his stay in Hyderabad, after we sisters were all married and he had retired from Bombay, he met Jassi Man Singh, wife of a Lieutenant General of the army, at a bookstore. She was asking for some titles which the store did not have. Knowing the craving a book lover feels, Daddy spoke to her and told her he had all those books, and if she would give him her address, he would post them to her. She did, and Daddy sent her all those and some more titles too, and they became friends forever, exchanging books, writing to each other and sharing experiences, so much so that in his last few years she visited him every few months, for her daughter was working at a project in Sitla in the Kumaon hills. She thought nothing of the rum filled air in his room while they chatted, and I noticed that when she needed to smoke, Daddy got out an ashtray from his cupboard. Surprised, I asked him later, and he said, "I respect the need of my friends to do whatever they wish. When we were younger, they would go for a stroll when they had to smoke; now they are all old, so I allow them the comfort of enjoying their puff right here.

One should not be fanatical, one should respect everyone's preferences." And I realised why he was so loved; he did not pretend, he actually respected all people! It was sad that some years later, Jassi's lovely daughter, Una, and her baby daughter both lost their lives, right there in Sitla, savouring the local mushrooms, which were actually poisonous and grew wild along with the healthy ones. Alas! Even Una's husband, Dr Sushil could not save them. They are still fondly remembered by the local people.

Since his college days, Daddy, along with his twin brother Trilochan had joined the Communist Party, and till his death he remained a dedicated Comrade. He had tremendous faith in Leninism and the policies of Karl Marx, though it is ironical that he was a successful entrepreneur. Trilochan uncle and Daddy had started a new business in Bombay, importing spare parts for trucks, buses and cars. Over three to four years they did quite well, so it was decided that Mummy and I, with my younger sister Bamboo should join Daddy there, for he had taken a house on rent. So in 1956, Mummy, 'Mataji' (my grandmother) and we two sisters, travelled to Bombay.

Bombay was full of the big-city glamour and excitement —everything was bigger and brighter; even the small corner 'Irani Hotel' felt like a very big joint, for it sold ice-cream, and even had a juke-box playing music. Haldwani was a one-street town but in Bombay, at every street corner there was a choice of three more roads to explore! We lived in the suburbs, in Khar, and most sojourns were to the Khar Municipal Market, where for the first time in my life I learnt that we had to pay for food. We would sometimes visit relatives who lived in Santa-Cruz. My school was also in Santa Cruz and we walked to school every day.

Bombay suburbs were not all concrete jungles then. Most houses in our lane were cottages, some Gujarati style and some Parsee style, and all had flowers and fruits growing in the compound. Coconut was mandatory, followed by Jamun and Badaam. Some people had chickoo trees, and one of my friends even had a cashew tree—that's the only time I've seen a cashew fruit; it was like an upside-down capsicum, with the cashew growing at the bottom, shaped like a comma, green in the beginning but gradually ripening into a brown kernel. While walking to school in the mornings, my friends and I would peep into the compound of the corner house to see if some almonds had fallen in the night. We would feel happy just seeing them fallen on the ground and walk away. Sometimes the lady of the house would call us back and give each of us a badaam or two, which we'd suck and chew on as we walked.

Some nearby streets were even less inhabited. There was lots of vacant land with some houses in between. The famous 'Linking Road' did not exist then and that area was a vast expanse of green. Near the sea-shore, the coconut palms grew tall and thick. The guys selling 'Chana Zor Garam' have nearly disappeared from Bombay. These were quaint people in tight pyjamas and loose frock-shaped shirts, Rajasthani style, who sold spicy fried gram seeds from small containers, spicing them according to the taste of the customer, selling the smallest packet for just ten paisa. They sang the 'Chana Zor Garam' song so throatily that you could hear them as they turned into your street, giving you enough time to cajole your mother to give you the money, and run out to your gate in time. The song has been immortalised by Manoj Kumar in his film 'Kranti', else for kids today it would be another legend grandmas talk about!

Fish entered our lives in a big way in Bombay. We started having fried fish at dinner every day. The vast variety, juicy taste and strong flavours of different kinds of fish, left us amazed as did the fisherwomen who sold it, with their colourful nine yard 'kashta' saris and thick gold chains and earrings.

The fish markets were noisy places with women chattering constantly among themselves in Marathi. They would bargain aggressively with the customers sometimes enticing them with English words like "fresh fish madam." Although they were competitors, yet there was a friendly atmosphere around.

Mummy and Daddy made many friends, and we would have lovely tea parties, and grand dinners when whole families got together and celebrated with gorgeous food, particularly chicken and fish, and great desserts. People in Bombay were way more advanced; they were already enjoying Chinese food and learning to cook it, baking lovely cakes, and experimenting with European cuisine. Mummy's cooking was particularly popular for she cooked exotic Persian dishes, full of butter and rich cream, using plums instead of tomatoes, in addition to other nuts and raisins. Many of these friends had travelled to Europe and America, and picked up quite a lot of western culture too. These ladies wore sleeveless blouses or dresses, and lived uninhibited lives, enjoying whatever their men enjoyed, be it clubbing, dancing, or even drinking! They drank their gin and lime juice with as much pleasure as the men did their scotch, though I used to wonder where it all came from, considering the prohibition! One particular dinner party held on our rooftop simply defied Indian culture. There was this lady called Neera, who had been Daddy's childhood friend in Nainital, but was now in Bombay married to a rich industrialist; she was hosting a party to celebrate their wedding anniversary, and asked Mummy to help her. Mummy took me along. Neera said they were not going to have children at this party, but Mummy said she could not leave me alone at home. I was surprised that Neera aunty had no servants to help her at the party, though her home was full of them. There were twelve couples who came, and while the drinks and snacks were served she got them all to play games she had devised for the evening. She would pull out slips with names written on them. It was always a male and a female called out together, and then she chose a punishment for them, which made everyone double up with laughter, but which I could not understand, though I could see Mummy and Daddy getting uncomfortable. So I pretended to have fallen asleep on the couch, to prevent them feeling embarrased. After the dessert, she got out a bowl in which everyone had left their car keys when they had arrived. She called the ladies one by one to be blindfolded and asked them to pick up one of the keys. Then the gentleman whose car key it was came up and bowed to the lady, after which they walked out together. I was so intrigued! I never told Mummy what I had seen, keeping up the sleeping pretence while Mummy helped Neera aunty to put away the crockery and food. But many years later when I knew better, she affirmed that it had indeed been a wife swapping event!

The political scene was also more vibrant and varied. In Haldwani everyone eulogised about the great Congress party, as U.P. had contributed the maximum number of Congressmen to the party, and Govind Ballabh Pant was the local and national hero. In Bombay, Daddy had friends from so many political parties. One of his friends, who was the P.A. to Sri Rajagopalachary, the first Viceroy of free India, was a Congressman, but his wife was a member of the Praja

Socialist Party. Even the Communists were of many hues—some were called Marxists, some southern Communists had different ideologies, some were called Socialists — for me it was all very confusing but Daddy would enjoy everyone's company.

Sadly, within a year we had to return to Haldwani from Bombay due to a major tragedy. We lost my younger sister, affectionately called Bamboo to Meningitis, for which there was no cure then. She was just past her third birthday, and I lovingly remember that she had just started going to school. She was amazingly pretty—all pink and chubby—and always cheerful. Her death left us all heartbroken and we just could not stay on in Bombay. I realise now that the pattern was already in place — whenever we were upset or sad or simply could not take it any more—we just tended to ship ourselves to Haldwani. It is so with me even today! And I swear it works. There's this interesting episode. Some years back, my son's friend, Mayank Tewari, now a famous script writer, but then a struggling correspondent with Hindustan Times, came to meet me. He was quite a few beers down and said to me, "Aunty please let me sit and cry on your shoulder, for tonight, I'm all shattered, I don't want to live any more, there's nothing to live for." I asked him what had happened and he said, "My girl friend just left me," and his tears would not stop. After a while I told him, "Will you do what I tell you, no questions asked." He said "Yes", and

I told him to rush to the bus Terminal and take the night bus to Nainital where he had a tiny hillside cottage, for a week. He came back a week later, full of cheer, with a new girl friend in tow!

I had come to Haldwani from Bombay, as I've said we had to, but the school in Bombay had admitted me in class 3rd according to my age. But Bauji was disappointed. He said, "You're going to be eight next year and you'll only be in class 4." One day, a lady came to our house and was waiting with the people outside to meet Bauji. He was the Municipal Commissioner of Haldwani, and many people approached him every day for help in many ways ; somebody's petition was stuck, somebody needed an arbitration, but most folks wanted jobs, specially Government jobs, and Bauji's help in getting them. This young lady told him that she had just finished her BA, which was a great thing for ladies to do at that time, and requested him to arrange for a government job. He thought for a while, then told her he would look into it it, but first, he asked her if she could teach me for a month, five hours a day. He offered her a salary of Rs. Sixty. She agreed. He instructed her to teach me the whole course for Hindi, English and Maths recommended for class Four, in one month. She was happy teaching me and being with us practically the whole day, as I was an avid learner. In the evening she took me for a walk, and pointed out the beautiful colours of nature. She taught me to admire all the flowers, and not to take them for granted; how the red of each flower was different, each buttercup was a different shade of yellow, and how, from afar, the buttercups looked like the earth smiling at the sun with a million little faces! She taught me what the homing birds meant to their little ones waiting in their tiny nests; how the different birds came and went with the seasons, how nature kept recycling everything through the thousands of insects and worms at work on different sites of decay, of which we could see plenty as most people defecated in the open woods. I was reminded of that important lesson last year on a visit to Innsbruck in Austria. An International Seminar on 'Ants' was being held for two days! The month just flew by, and at the end of it Bauji asked the Principal of the school, Mrs Tiku, to arrange to take my exams for class four. Of course I passed, and she promoted me to class Five. That year I studied for the first half in Haldwani, and the second half in a small school called,'The Rose Manor Garden School' in Bombay, getting transferred to high school in class six. Thus it came about that before my ninth birthday, I was in class six at the St. Teresa's Convent School, Santa Cruz, Bombay.

☺☹☺

Chapter 4

St Teresa's Convent School

St Teresa's is situated on the Ghod Bunder Road, now called the S V Road which is the main artery of the city, linking the South to the North of Bombay, particularly the airport to the main city. Those days, anything beyond Dadar was the 'suburbs'. The school was quite big even then, and has since kept growing. The main gate opens into grounds, but it is the side gate which is generally used. This gate leads to the most beautiful grotto of Mother Mary and Baby Jesus that I have ever seen. I still get to see it in many Hindi films that have been shot in the school, and it's still the same. Opposite the grotto, there is a small cottage which is the Principal's Office Block. It is very impressively decorated with fish-tanks, and stuffed birds, some very rare. We also had huge halls with theatrically painted stages, where we had Assembly when it rained.

I was gradually exposed to the social structure of the school, and marvelled at what I saw. There were girls who travelled to school by local trains from as far off as 'Bassein', an hour's journey. There were lots of girls who had come to study from Goa, as there were only a few good schools there. Some of these girls stayed in the small school hostel but most stayed with relatives. Goa was then Portuguese territory, so every vacation these girls left for their 'country', and came back to 'India' in June, flaunting European chocolates or pencils, or other presents, which were not available in Bombay. There were daughters of very rich and powerful people—Film producers, mill-owners, police commissioners, ministers, even a few actresses who worked in commercial Hindi films; and there were also girls whose parents could not afford their fees, or books or uniforms. The classes simply melted away and all of us students were absolutely at ease with each other. If a rich student acted haughty, others would at once correct her, for no one tolerated haughtiness or bad manners.

A very delightful aspect of our school was that whoever landed at the Bombay airport HAD to pass by our school on the way to the city. Thus we got to see several dignitaries who visited Bombay. Our Principal would queue us up outside the school and arrange for the VIP vehicles to slow down or even stop for a minute, so that we could see them, cheer them and wave at them. The visit of the Queen Elizabeth II, in nineteen sixty one with Lord Mountbatten and Princess

Margaret is most unforgettable, as also that of President John F. Kennedy with Jacqueline. They all came standing in open jeeps, smiling and waving at the crowds and looking extremely beautiful—so elegantly dressed—they looked so glamorous. The only Indian lady I have seen, who came close to these personalities in beauty and grace was Mrs Vijaylaxmi Pandit, Jawaharlal Nehru's sister and a politician in her own right. She was the Governor of Bombay, and later the Ambassador to Britain. Nehru, whom \we saw from our school gate in an open jeep, was also very handsome but his personality lacked their cheerfulness; he seemed to scowl under the weight of his responsibilities.

It so happened that when John F Kennedy came to visit India, a bullet-proof car had been shipped to India from the USA especially for his use. But when he was returning, he left the car behind as a gift for Mother Teresa, who was doing great social work with her Missionaries of Charity. After dropping President Kennedy at the Santa Cruz airport, the car was parked in our school compound for about a week, after which Mother Teresa came to take its delivery. My most prized moment is when I met her in person. She told us that food was very valuable and that we should not waste any. Instead, we should all try to make do with a little less, and try to feed the needy. She spoke about her work, and about how her nuns would visit the airport and request the air-hostesses not to throw away the leftover food served during the flights, but put it in a bag for her poor, things like uneaten sandwiches, or fruits, or even the small packets of sugar and jam. She was a true saint. She lived every moment of her life with God's name on her lips, and the benefit of the poor on her mind. Such people are very rare. Later we learnt that the Presidential car had been auctioned for twelve lakh rupees, and the money used for the poor.

When the Archbishop of Canterbury came visiting, and later Pope John from the Vatican, they stopped their open cars near our school gate, and all the nuns had the good fortune to see them up close, and kiss the Papal ring too!

Another unique experience at St Teresa's was that we had the daughter of Mr B R Chopra, a prominent Hindi film producer, studying with us. Mr Chopra gave Hindi cinema the best films for several years, and he was kind enough to send across his films to our nuns to screen them for students! I remember seeing the film, 'Boot Polish' in school. The actress 'Baby Naaz' was also a student of our school at that time. We would be taken to the hall, where the Sisters put up a projector and screen, and we sat on the floor and watched the films, rapt with wonder, as many of us had not gone to the cinema before. Later I remember seeing the films 'Sujata', 'Madhumati' and even 'Mere Mehboob'. The last was shown only to those of us who had passed in all the subjects. We would turn to look curiously at the nuns whenever there was a romantic scene, for they would duly cover their eyes. So cute!

As I progressed to the higher classes, I began to take part in elocution competitions, debates, and loved doing Hindi one-act plays.

In the fifties our business in Bombay was flourishing and daddy was doing well. By my ninth birthday we had got a new Ambassador car, Trilochan uncle had been blessed with a son, and Mom and Dad with another got a daughter, 'Pappu', eight years my junior. They loved her to a fault for she made up for Bamboo's loss.

Daddy now had innumerable friends. The weekend political discussions were euphoric and optimistic. Bombay being the industrial and commercial capital of India, having the maximum number of textile mills, was almost taken over by Socialist and Communist parties, the Trade Union Movement being their field of operations. Dhage and George Fernandez were the new political heroes, and daddy loved it when the profits were shared by the workers.

Over the next few years I learnt a lot. I dug into my studies and whatever the subject, I gave it my best. My Dad taught me how to 'read' well, how to feel the metre in poetry and also in prose, which made me 'feel' and 'love' the language. I avidly read many books. My first book was The Man-eaters of Kumaon by Jim Corbett. I told Dad it was too long for me to read, and he gave me the Mantra, that I follow till today— "Read the first twenty pages. If the book retains your interest, read it through, but don't give up before at least twenty pages."

When I reached class seven, I didn't want to learn History; I only wanted English, Hindi and Maths. Dad made the History book so interesting for me, that I read and learnt the whole book in the first month of the school year! This passion for reading History lasted through my college years and for several years after that too.

Marathi was a big no-no for me, and I did not pass in it in my sixth Std. At that time Bauji was in Bombay and he did something wonderful. He was seeing a local doctor, Dr Trilokikar for some problem, and made the good doctor a strange request; he asked him if his brother's wife, who was a home-maker, could spend an hour or two with me every day, just speaking with me in Marathi. Thus, over the next three months, I learnt to speak Marathi well, after which the language was no problem. This is how my grooming was contributed to by every member of the family.

Trilochan uncle helped me learn French in class ten. He advised me to read aloud, paying attention to the pronunciation, even if I could not understand them. I persevered for a few months, and automatically began to get the language and grammar right. Again the method of 'feeling' and 'absorbing' 'what you read! Looking back, it surprises me that there was no pressure for scoring marks, learning was for my own satisfaction. What mattered to Daddy was that I should be reading, and reading good books. There was a bookshop near Khar Railway Station, 'V L Nayak and

Co', where Dad had given instructions that I could pick up anything without the need to ask the price! Dad would pay. So all new and old books and magazines were lapped up.

Books taught me about life, about people, about acceptance, and became my emotional crutch later in life. I felt that nothing was impossible, that knowledge gave you an edge over everything. In fact on page one of every book, I wrote, "Knowledge is power." Late in life I realised, "Knowledge is proud that it knows so much, wisdom is humble that it knows no more!"

When I joined St Teresa's, and walked into class six, I politely asked my teacher where I should sit. Seeing my height, she told me to sit in the last row. Soon I began to realize what it was to be a back bencher; all the girls who were not interested in studying, or were repeating the class, would sit in the last two rows of the class, and occupy a world all of their own. They would be whispering jokes to each other, planning pranks, having fun; coming to attention only when their names were called by the teacher, then the girl called would stand up sheepishly and pretend that she could not hear clearly what the teacher had said, or that the blackboard was shining and she could not see what was written on it. I was amazed at this wily lot; I thought if I could see and hear everything clearly, why couldn't they? Gradually the teacher noticed that I was attentive and sincere, so she moved me to the corner seat in the first row. But in every new class, in the beginning I was allotted the last row, as I kept growing taller. Some girls were very mischievous. Once they sprinkled ink on the skirts of some girls, and passed on the blame to others. Another time they stuck bubblegum on the seats of two girls sitting in front.

When the girls sat down unsuspecting they got glued to the seats. When they tried to stand up to answer the roll call, they could not. It was hilariously funny. Their skirts had to be cut where the gum had stuck, and they walked home with holes in their skirts. The eighth Std. back benchers were sneaking in pictures of Cliff Richards, Ricky Nelson and other film heroes, and exchanging them, and even kissing them. Ugh! They hero worshipped film stars and cricketers. One of these girls, Monica, showed me her photographs where she was heavily painted and looked very different and grown-up, though quite attractive. She told me she had to spend a lot of money getting these pictures made as she had to give them to her 'agent' who got her work. She did small roles in films. I could not understand how the bad world of films and the 'good' world of school co-existed in her life!

In class ninth and tenth we shifted to the new building from where one could look down and see the lovely cottages of the colony alongside our boundary wall. During the lunch hour I'd see a few of our school girls talking with some boys from the neighbouring Sacred Heart boys school. Some held hands; some walked arm in arm. When I showed this to the other girls, they would snort, "Ha! If you ask any one of them, she'll say it was her brother or cousin. Forget them." Phyllis Mendez, one of the back-benchers was very tall, at least 5 ft. 10 inches. She had very long and slim straight legs that were very hairy before she began to shave them, thin long arms; actually a thin tall body, with curly cropped hair, and a nondescript face, eyes hidden behind thick glasses, a long neck around which she wore a cross, and a dull brown complexion; an unattractive person for all of us, for she was never friendly and was always a loner. I learnt years later that she had gone to France to try for a job for she had a friend there. The great designer Christian Dior chanced to see her somewhere, and was delighted with her body. After that for almost two decades, he designed clothes with only Phyllis as his muse, and with all the beauty treatments etc, she did look pretty. She gained poise and confidence and looked very stylish. But sadly she never made any real friends, and after the death of Christian Dior, ended her life, committing suicide in a hotel room in Bombay.

I got a peep into the lifestyle of some of my other schoolmates. When I had to dress up for a play to be performed in school, a friend offered to get my make-up done by a specialist from the famous R K Studios, as her father worked there. When I went to her house for the make-up, I asked for her parents as I wanted to greet them, and she told me, "they're in the garden making love!" Seeing my scandalized look, she said, "Oh you! They're in the garden having tea and biscuits and perhaps sharing a kiss, but we tease them like this when they are in the garden together." And I thought of the dozen frowns I would get at home if I related this episode to my prudish U P family! But I really liked this bold and brash family; they were smart and led colourful lives, were witty and totally fitted the current word, 'bindaas'. My best friend was Komal, a very sensitive and soft person, with whom I was inseparable. I began to shed many inhibitions, and enlarged my vocabulary to include many hitherto unmentionable words.

What changed my whole perception was an incident that happened in class ten. Geetanjali Mahendroo too was a good friend, and we often visited each other to play or simply chat. My family knew her family. She was the niece of the famous music director Madan Mohan, Though she wasn't much into studies, we enjoyed playing, chatting and walking together. One night Mom and Dad went to the 'Gazebo' for dinner. It was the first restaurant in the suburbs to have a live band, and they saw Geetanjali dancing there, 'night club style', and did not like it. The next morning, my mother ordered me to break the friendship with her as she was not a 'good girl'. Geeta went on to become a famous actor, Anju Mahendroo who was Rajesh Khanna's partner for eight years. The song in the film 'Daag' was put in to portray her pain when he dropped her. I appreciate the fact she is still doing meaningful roles, as the one in 'The Dirty Picture' recently.

The biggest scandal happened when I was in class ten. One of the class eleven girls suddenly disappeared. For a week no one talked about her, as if even having known her could get them into trouble. The word got round, "A young eleventh standard student of St Teresa's has gone missing!" Even Daddy started talking of sending me back to Nainital to study. After a week, everything became clear. It transpired that this girl was a huge fan of the actor Dev Anand. Since she lived in Juhu and her father had a hotel in Juhu, and Dev Anand also lived in Juhu, she often approached his driver to arrange for her to meet the actor. Everytime, they would make plans which didn't work out, so they kept meeting and making better plans, till they both fell madly in love with each other. And now they had eloped. It was 1963 and families were very conservative. They never expected their parents to agree to the match. Anyway, within a week her father traced them. He acted very wisely; he actually got them married, and installed his son-in-law as the new manager of his hotel. The girl finally got to meet her idol, for Dev Anand was gracious enough to attend the wedding of his ex-employee.

Chapter 5

Some Family and Social History

Things at home were different now. After Bamboo went, *Bauji's* elder brother's wife whom we called '*Taiji*' also expired. She had been the most loving of all the people in the house—quiet, calm, and very hard-working. My earliest memories of her are of her being up at four in the morning, churning an earthen pot full of curds to get the butter out. A big wooden churner was in place on the mouth of the '*matka*', and *Taiji* would be pulling at a rope alternatively with both hands to rotate it, at the same time reciting her morning prayers. During the day she would cook goodies for us, or embroider. We still use some of her embroidered sheets. It was remarkable that she never traced or planned a pattern, but starting from one corner of the sheet, went on creating designs, simply by counting the threads of the cotton weave of the fabric, and by the time she embroidered around the whole sheet, her design would converge and align with the beginning of the work with mathematical precision. She showed me how the famous '*Phulkaris*' of Punjab were created. First tufts of pure cotton were rolled through a '*Charkha*', that has been made immortal by Gandhiji, to spin a uniform yarn. Then the bundles of yarn were woven into a sheet and dyed in the brick red colour using natural dyes, the colour of which would never fade. Then different shades of silken yarn were used to create a perfect mathematical pattern, embroidering from the reverse side of the cloth, counting the threads, while the pattern appeared on the front side. I still have a couple of these almost indestructible sheets called '*Baagh*', and I used them for the wedding ceremonies of my sons and my guests were duly impressed. Beside this, Taiji had perfected the craft of spinning silken cords, and watching her at it both intrigued and delighted me. One cot was tilted up against a wall, and some fine silk yarn tied lengthwise between its two shorter frames. Then with a pen sized stick with another yarn tied to it, her hand went right to left, and left to right, doing what I could not fathom, but by evening, a soft but strong cord had been woven, with a few inches of leftover yarn tied at the end in a decorative fringe. These were proudly worn by both men and women, some people even let a couple of inches be seen from under their shirts, to flaunt their "*Reshmi Naala*", a fancy hand woven silken cord to tie the pyjamas of well-off men and women (and we think Fashion is a recent phenomenon). Taiji had amazing talent, and a quiet and peaceful demeanour, but great inner strength.

My grandfather attributed all his success to her, and revered her as his mother. His younger sister Inder Kaur's husband died when she had been married for just a year as she entered her teens. Traditionally, in Punjab, young and even not so young widows are automatically married to the younger brother of the deceased husband. Inder Buaji's husband had four younger brothers, and according to the custom prevailing in Punjab, her in-laws wanted her to remarry and settle with one of them. This custom is actually a great social benefactor, especially when the families are financially just, well, modest; as it takes care of the widow and her needs, and of her children, if any, in a graceful and honourable way—even brothers already married are known to take on their brothers' widows as second wives, and look after their social, economic, and physical needs. It also helps avoid any succession disputes, with the land and other wealth remaining in the family.

Now Tayaji was a very rich man, socially and politically well placed. He said that had his father been alive, he may have gladly allowed the remarriage to happen. But he, being the elder brother, would not allow it, lest society taunt him for not being able to support his widowed sister. So Buaji came home with him, and lived on to hit a century almost. She was around to take care of my two elder kids, Chingi and Ricky, who grew up under her care. She was also there to bless Chintu, my third son, but went just before Babboo, my youngest was born. Just as Taiji was meek and benevolent and totally unassuming, Buaji was dynamite, with the ignition on! They say that she was a fireball. Even when she was young she is said to have fought with Tayaji, who was elder to her, when he did not allow her to remarry. She actually quarrelled with him for having remarried when his first wife died, and living with his new wife in marital bliss, but not allowing her to do the same. She did try to assert her rights, and her arguments were justified. But Tayaji, with his obstinacy and haughty snob values turned around and said, "Ok, even my wife will live with you and my mother in the village, while I pursue my business in Kathgodam!" The village was 'Lathiphal' in the Rawalpindi District of pre- partitioned India. Around that time his other sister died and her husband remarried. Tayaji was very concerned about the care of her orphaned son Manohar. He brought the child home, and handed him over to Buaji to bring up and this fulfilled her craving for a family of her own. This was Manohar uncle. At that time Tayaji was a major construction contractor for the Government, and had built the first railway station of Kathgodam, when the railway lines were laid.

India was then being ruled by the British, who could

not tolerate the tropical heat here. They developed several hill-stations like Mussoorie near Dehradun, Nainital, Simla, Dalhousie and others, where they could escape to in the peak heat of summer. The whole government paraphernalia shifted to the hill-stations during summer. In Kashmir, the winter capital of the state was Jammu and the summer capital was Srinagar. Almost all ministries from Delhi shifted to Simla in the summer months. Likewise in the United Provinces or UP, the state capital shifted from Lucknow to Nainital. The whole contract for shifting the government offices to Nainital and back, came to Tayaji, and it was a very big deal, requiring numerous vehicles and lots of staff. All the ministers, civil servants and officers, down to the peons had to be transported to Nainital and back and all relevant files and documents too. So Tayaji was not only in the ministers' good books, but he also made a lot of money. Bauji being his younger brother was educated in English at home by a British pastor, and was later sent to Agra Medical College to study Medicine. As luck would have it, Tayaji expired before Bauji could complete his course. Since Tayaji had no offspring, Taiji announced that Bauji was now the successor to S Teja Singh. Accordingly Bauji left his studies just a year before graduation, and came to Kathgodam to take over the flourishing business.

He expanded the business to newer heights, and his social and political standing was unrivalled. He created lots of jobs for the local people; the 'Paharis', and they loved him in return. They were in awe of him. It was the perfect fusion—on one hand he was rubbing shoulders with the wealthiest, dressed like the British in excellently tailored suits, sparkling white shirts and shining leather shoes, complete with a silver pocket watch—on the other hand his home was run in the Indian tradition where the women kept 'purdah', cooked the food themselves, and were pious. The clincher was that while he spoke the King's language to perfection with the officials, he spoke to the locals in chaste 'Pahari'. He never let their concerns go unattended. The government soon appointed him the 'Municipal Commissioner' of Haldwani, a position he held till 1955, when it was decided by the Indian government that the post had to be filled by an elected person. Persevered upon by the people of Haldwani, he even contested that election and won, and was the Municipal Commissioner for another five years, after which he resigned.

In business he had good foresight and his strong personality got him through where lesser souls could not edge in. He began a new business of public transport for ferrying people to remote hill towns and villages of Kumaon, as the region is now called. Sardar Vallabhai Patel had insisted upon building a good network of roads to link remote parts of the country, mainly the border regions; a lesson learnt during the battles fought with Pakistan when Kashmir had to accede to India in 1947. More roads meant more transport, and more vehicles. He also bought his own petrol pumps, for which dealerships were being sold by the Standard Vacuum Co. His friend from Bombay, Mr Nariman, bought nearly a hundred pumps, in different towns from Kathgodam to Bareilly, Moradabad and other cities, but Bauji wisely took only two which he could control well. The Nainital bank had also come up and Bauji was a major shareholder and a Director in the bank's Managing Committee. I remember when I was about six years old, he took me along for a board-meeting at the bank. When halfway through the meeting I got hungry, he sent the peon to get bananas for me, and the meeting resumed only after I had eaten the bananas, and convinced him that I was hungry no more!

In our community, among the Sikhs, Bauji became a towering figure in our region. He contributed in every way to the progress of the community. The first half of the twentieth century was very important for the Sikhs. For nearly a century they had been hounded by Muslim rulers, who wanted them to be uprooted completely. There was a price on every Sikh head—anyone who killed a Sikh was rewarded with eighty rupees, a large sum of money those days. So people hunted Sikhs, both men and women. Legends of Sikhs sleeping on their mounts, holding a branch of a tree, ready to flee upon the scent of danger are actually true! For decades devout Sikhs lived in jungles, fighting lonely battles, protecting the tenets of Sikhism in the form of their garb, and the Sikh scriptures. People leading to the arrest of Sikhs were also highly rewarded, but a very strong and secret set of Sikhs managed to keep the religion alive.

The middle of the nineteenth and beginning of the twentieth century however saw a major revival, and their numbers grew multi-fold. Punjab had been under Sikh rule with Maharaja Ranjit Singh, who brought glory to the whole community and also resurrected the places of worship, the 'Gurudwaras'. Later the British army also encouraged Sikhism and favoured Sikhs in every field. Primarily, Sikhs in Punjab were a farming race, happy with the canal laying the government had initiated, for what more does a farmer want but ample and timely water supply for his fields. A contented peasantry was also favourable for the British. Since the Mutiny of 1957, they were looking for an alternative to both Hindus and Muslims, who had had an issue with the pig-fat being used for lubricating their guns. Sikhs had no such taboos, so they began to be given more and more recruitment in the army. They were also stronger, tougher, healthier, more disciplined and honest, with few demands.

The British also encouraged the Sikhs to follow their religion and the teachings of their Gurus, by building Gurudwaras in their cantonments, and hiring 'Granthis', or priests to work for propagating the religion, to keep them inspired and motivated, for their Gurus were themselves

'Saint-Soldiers'. It worked for everyone, and both the British and the Sikhs remained in each others' good books. By the end of the British rule, Sikhs formed 57% of the Indian Army, having fought valiantly along with the British soldiers across the globe, in Europe, South Africa and Japan. All over the Punjab, which was then from Panipat and Pathankot to Peshawar, almost every Hindu family converted at least one child to Sikhism. The faith became very popular, and people were proud to be a 'Guru ka Sikh'. As Sikhs grew wealthier, they began to improve the structures of the Gurudwaras, and to search for and take possession of those Gurudwaras which were usurped, or lost previously. These became like small forts, where everybody converged for safety in distress, for community festivities and other religious activities, and majorly for free 'Prasad' and 'Langar' or food from the community kitchen.

Bauji too, along with some like-minded people, began to work towards these goals. He bought land in Kathgodam, a hundred yards from the railway station, and built the first Gurudwara in that region. It became very popular and everyone visited it at least once a day.

Soon he bought a huge orchard in Haldwani in 'Bhotia Parao', where he built a house for the family. Up till then only my grandmother whom we called 'Mataji', was living in Kathgodam and Nainital with my father and uncle, both twins. Buaji, Taiji, and Bauji's own mother were living in

Lathiphal, looking after the 'Zamindari'. Now the whole family shifted to this new house, the one with the huge tamarind tree, a landmark house for me. Bauji also bought land in Haldwani town to build a Gurudwara there. This plot was opposite the only huge ground called the 'Ramlila Ground', The plan was to have the Gurudwara for regular prayers, and to use the Ramlila Ground for 'Kirtans' and Langar on ceremonial days.

There is an interesting story about how this was achieved. It seems the area next to the Gurudwara plot was home to nautch girls and prostitutes, whose patrons were powerful people — politicians and other leaders. It did not suit them to have a Gurudwara next to their quarters, for their clientele would vanish, not being able to get the privacy and secrecy needed when visiting these shady areas. So they used their clout with the authorities to stay the permission for the Gurudwara to be built.

After several attempts at obtaining legal permission, and having failed, Bauji and his friends devised an alternative plan. They encircled the plot with a boundary of long wooden planks tied together and left it for some days. After some days, when it was least expected, some labourers worked quietly through the night and built a small room, about ten feet by twenty feet, with a tin corrugated sheet roof, and a door and a window, in one corner of the plot. Early in the morning before sunrise, the 'Guru Granth

Sahib' was installed there and the reciting of prayers and Kirtan began. No one guessed what was going on inside. On the date of the court hearing, it was brought to the notice of the court that the place had an existing and functional Gurudwara; and the law does not give anyone the right to demolish an existing place of worship! Thus the dissenters had to look for new addresses, and slowly a huge Gurudwara was built.

Since education for girls was a cause Sikhs believe in, a 'Khalsa School' for girls was started in the ground floor of the Gurudwara, of which Bauji was the chairman. The school grew very popular, so later he bought a plot of land, in Bhotia Parao, and the school was shifted there. Today, it is a huge campus where girls are studying up to post graduation with multi-faculties and programmes.

Since the 'Shiromani Gurudwara Management Committee' had taken control of the main Sikh shrines in Punjab and elsewhere, repairing and other construction work was being done at all historical places. The scriptures were being read more, analysed and researched and translated by a large number of scholars. Sikh history was being studied and published. It had come to light that some sixty-five kilometres from Haldwani was the historical place where Guru Nanak Devji had come during his sojourns, and had an important dialogue with the followers of the 'Gorakh Matt'. This place had historical importance for Sikhs, and

Bauji, with some friends decided to get it restored to the Sikh community, from the Gorakhs who had taken possession of the place. He used to recount how they used to go through the jungle in jeeps, with guns, to protect them from wild animals, and servants to cook and feed them, for without a road or known path, even those 65 km. could take days to cover.

Historians came from Punjab with written chronicles, and ascertained that there was proof that this was indeed the historical site, "Nanak Matta."

Thereupon Bauji engaged the services of Shri Gobind Ballabh Pant, an eminent lawyer who belonged to Haldwani, who went on to become the first Home Minister of independent India and who was also Bauji's friend, to file a suit in the High Court on behalf of the Sikhs, to retrieve the land that was historically theirs. He fought the case successfully, though it went on for several years, and ultimately the Allahabad High Court passed a judgement granting the ownership of the Gurudwara to the Sikhs, along with thirty square kilometres of its surrounding land! The woods were cleared and a new Gurudwara was built, fulfilling the labour of Bauji and his friends. Post independence, thousands of farmers from Punjab, and many who had had to leave their homes in the partitioned Pakistan, trailed to this fertile area, started farming after cutting down the woods; and changed the geography, the climate, ecology, demography and environment of the place forever. Starting from Nanak Matta to Bilaspur, nearly 200 sq. Km. of jungles were cut down to make way for cultivation. Today this region is called "Udham Singh Nagar," and is known for some of the most successful and rich Sikh farmers. It is alarming to realise the scant respect given to our forests and trees, compared to an incident when, a British magistrate in Nainital had sentenced a man who had cut down a fully grown pine tree, to a year of imprisonment. When the man protested, the magistrate said, "can you in your life time, give back to this hill another fully grown tree? This tree took nearly a hundred years to stand so tall."Here, woods were being cut so people could start farming, and in the hills, for an annual payment of some thousand rupees, acres upon acres of jungle were contracted to timber merchants to pull down the trees and cut them and sell them all over the country. Such simple rules, such fatal results for the environment! Tough lessons have since been learnt, that nature should be respected. Though what is happening now is not very different; for a few thousand rupees one could destroy thousands of trees, for a few hundred crores of rupees, now you can raze hundreds of Adivasi villages to get the coal out of their land.

The decade of the fifties was very lucky for Bauji. When India was partitioned in 1947, he had opened his arms to all the people coming in from what now became Pakistan.

He helped each person who approached him to settle in Haldwani or Nainital. He built small two roomed quarters at the back of our garden, with verandas in front, which he gave to the refugees coming back. He helped them to find jobs, and those who had money were helped to start new shops or other business. Some people with just a little money were encouraged to buy a bus in partnership with another and he would help them to get finance, and permits to ply the buses, and get routes allotted to them, so that they could earn a dignified and decent living. Soon everyone settled down with some occupation or the other. Some people who were wealthier, and had also been able to retrieve their money from Pakistan, purchased fleets of buses, seeing it as an easy and lucrative business. Then they began to create competition for the smaller operators, who had just one or two buses, by charging lesser fares. When this went on for some time, Bauji tried to control it by allotting lucrative routes to the smaller transporters, but it did not work. So he did something brilliant—he formed a co-operative of all transporters, called the 'Kumaon Motor Owners Union Ltd.', of which he was the founder-Chairman. The co-operative fixed the fares and the routes for all buses, and is till today a success story—their buses ply to far flung villages where often even State Transport buses cannot reach! I feel wonderful when I see a bus with 'K M O U Ltd' written on its wind-screen.

After that Bauji dealt with Housing. He demarcated the empty stretch of land from Tikonia to Bhotia Parao, up to our own boundary in fact and divided it into small and big plots, creating two housing colonies, "Guru Nanak Pura" and "Guru Gobind Pura." Then he called all the Sikhs who did not own their houses, to apply for the said plots, "I am still in power," he told them "I want all my community people to have their own houses. You can pay part of the money now, and then the rest slowly in small instalments." Even then the complacent folks had to be coaxed to take the step—that when the cost of the smaller plots was just Rs 200 and the bigger plot was Rs 500! Four adjacent plots were left alone to build a Sikh Temple later on.

Chapter 6

Trilochan Uncle

Trilochan uncle is my Dad's twin, and his only sibling. They cannot be told apart, their appearance, voice, gait, demeanour, all are identical. Both did an M A from Allahabad University, then Uncle continued there for his Law degree, and my father went to Christian College, Lucknow. They shared the same interests in reading, had common friends, and were each others' best friends too. Still, everything changes, and towards the end of his life, Daddy fell out with his brother. I keep wondering what could have caused so much bitterness in him, as by nature he was a kind person.

From class five onwards, our trips to Haldwani were limited to the summer holidays. En route to Haldwani, we would stop at Delhi for some days, so we could meet all the close relatives; it was very important back then. We'd spend some time with my '*Maasiji*' at Curzon Road, my Mom's sister. She had a huge two acre house with a vast lawn. Jagjit my cousin was my age, and was very affectionate, and 'Koko' my favourite friend, conscience-keeper, shoulder-to-lean-on is still close to me.

Uncle's wedding was a very enjoyable affair. Our whole house was decorated with fairy lights, specially brought in from Delhi. Lots of sweets were made fresh, and served. Evening meals were the best. All the ladies of the locality would gather in our house and sing Punjabi songs, using the melodious words to very wittily bring out the hypocrisy and wickedness, or the flirtatious nature of different relationships. It was all in fun and humour. After that the men would start dancing. They danced in circles, and with such vigour and energy that the ground shook with the power of their thumping feet, and we kids were advised to stand at a safe distance, lest we got accidently hurt. Time seemed to stop, actually. They went on for a long time, till slowly, they began to tire, and spun slower, and slower, and then flopped on the various cots, wiping their sweat. Even the '*Dhol Wallas*', or drummers, would go sit panting in a corner.

I felt so proud of these tall handsome '*sardars*' with their Punjabi vitality and immense stamina, and always wondered at the source of their energy! But no, I had actually seen these rustic people eating also. They would think nothing of devouring piles of Chapattis, with loads of mutton curry, and round it off with a plate full of *halwa*.

It was only decades later that another secret was revealed to me—the secret of all the scotch served quietly in *Bauji's* room! Having seen their appetite for food, I could only imagine that it must have flowed in buckets rather than bottles. All this pomp was justified, for besides *Bauji's* position in society, uncle was marrying the daughter of Mr Sucha Singh, the director of Firestone Tyres in India and the ceremony was held at a prestigious address at Delhi's Akbar Road!

Soon, Kuljit aunty was pregnant, and so was Mummy! And I was so excited to know that I would have two little siblings now. I prayed for a brother though it didn't matter to me if it was born to mummy or to aunty. The following year, aunty gave birth to a boy, right there in the house. I was in school. I was aware of the activity in the house since morning, the doctor being there, so when I heard a baby's cry, I rushed out from class, which was in Mrs. Tiku's part of the house then, saying "my brother has come!" Automatically, I became the master of ceremonies in the house, deciding who will be allowed to hold 'Tutu' as we called him. The joy the first grandson brought to the family was unparalleled!

Three weeks later, my second sister, Pappu was born in Nainital as Mummy needed special care, it being a 'breach' delivery. Mummy, Daddy and I were equally happy at Pappu's birth. She was very special for my parents. Trilochan Uncle took great care of Mummy after Daddy went away to Bombay. Uncle had four more children, three daughters and another son.

Chapter 7

'Mummu' – My Mother

My mother's story reads like a fable of a faraway princess! She was born in Quetta, an important town nestling in the Hindu- Kush ranges of mountains, in the state of Baluchistan, a part of undivided India, which became famous for the worst of reasons; the world's most devastating earthquake happened there in 1935. Her father had business interests in China, where he traded silk; in Bombay, where he had built a market place, letting out the shops to different traders; in Karachi, where he had his head office and a big house; and then across the western border's in Iran, where he had been 'outsourced' the construction work for the Iranian Army. He had built the cantonment in Seistan in Iran, with rows of barracks and many other installations. He led scores of his friends and relatives to Iran, and they all made a fortune there; some of these people traded in dry fruits, some in motor spare parts, some in fabrics, according to their calling. Many of them made Teheran their home. Mom, in her childhood, in the early thirties, experienced such exotic places like the famous Anarkali Bazaar of Lahore, the buzzing markets of Karachi, which even had a harbour for shipping goods, and the beautiful and peaceful Iran which was a rich country under the rule of Shah Pehelvi. Before shifting to Dehradun, she had already learnt horse-riding and swimming in the chilly streams of Kashmir where her elder sister lived; and archery and a little bit of sword-fighting in Iran. The sword fascinated her, as it was the symbol of Sikh bravery, and Mom was very brave; even her name '*Daler*' meant 'the fearless one'! While in college in Dehradun, she was a member of the '*Prantiya Raksha Dal*', something like N C C today, and learnt rifle-shooting, and won prizes in it too. She could milch a buffalo, kneeling down with a pail between her knees both hands tight on the udders or go racing through town on her bicycle with equal ease.

Daddy did none of these, but Mom unabashedly rode around Dehradun with him sitting pillion on the bar of her bicycle, before she taught him to ride it. She was tall, slim and very beautiful, and the colour red suited her vibrant personality. Above all, she loved people. Before she came to Dad's family, she gave so much love to all her cousins that they remember her fondly even today. After coming into Dad's family, she embraced everyone equally and loved them. Those of his cousins who were not good in studies, she brought them to live in our house, and tutored them herself. So I grew up with dozens of cousins, learning different things from her; some would be learning Maths, some English, some History; even sewing and embroidery for the marriageable young girls. Consequently everyone was eager to please me and do things for me, but she discouraged them and taught me to be fiercely independent. When she recounted her experiences of the various places she had lived in, I would be fascinated, and it certainly broadened my vision from a very young age, but she never flaunted her interesting past to Dad's relatives. How they all respected her!

Mom and Dad were both very generous. They gave away things constantly. Dad gave thousands of rupees to a friend who was building a house saying, "he is building his own home for the first time, he should not get discouraged!" I now realize that in a running business, a few ups and downs get taken care of, and when I see the happiness and contentment and security Dad's old friend is enjoying because he has his own house, I thank God for such a kind father. There is another memory of his kindness and wisdom. It happened in Bombay when I must have been six or seven years old. Dad's friend, Pushp Raj, came over to our house with his girl friend, and poured out his story about not being allowed to marry the girl he loved—how cruel his parents were! He wanted Daddy to help him get married to her, and convince his parents and hers too. Dad instead told him that if he wanted to marry he would first have to be earning independently. Since he was only a graduate, Dad convinced him to join the Law College. Financially his parents would not support him as they wanted him to join the family business. Dad told him that he would take care of everything. He gave him all the law books he needed, and even taught him, and helped him complete the course. After that, when he had joined a law firm, he asked him to marry the young girl, who was faithfully waiting for him. "Now you are fit to support a family, financially and socially. Marry and be happy. You should marry only when you are confident of giving ample financial comforts to your wife. There is no point in marrying, and then living a life compromising on the standard of living that you are used to." I remember when I had just joined college, we were invited to a grand party at Pushp Raj's posh Marine Drive apartment, when he was appointed a judge to Bombay High Court. At the party he acknowledged that he had achieved all that he did, because of dad's wise guidance!

Sadly, even the best of families fall into petty social traps. The pressure to have a son was immense those days. For Mom it was sad that she had three daughters, and though we were loved and even brought up like sons—we were not sons! The craving for a son, the insecurity of not having a son—how can I call it an evil of those times, when it is very much there even today? I have seen my own granddaughters praying for a brother, before my grandsons were born. Some things never change; at least those days daughters were allowed to be born, unlike now. The stress began to tell on Mom's happiness and health too for she was very sensitive.

It was sad for Mom, and she kept losing her health as she developed Asthma. More debilitating than Asthma were the medicines she had to take; they took their toll and she went away very soon. After we sisters were married, Mom, Dad and Gullu shifted to Hyderabad, which was peaceful and had a good climate. Mom spent three happy years there. But nobody has any business to go away the way she did! She was having her evening tea with Dad. When he finished his tea he saw that she had not finished hers. When he asked her, she said, "See what's happening to me." Dad thought it was the Asthma and began to rub her back. A minute later, she said, "Oh! They've come." Then she took God's name, and with her head on Dad's shoulder, passed away! She was just fifty one, without a single streak of grey in her hair.

☺☺☹

Chapter 8

Snakes In Haldwani

Living in Haldwani, on the edge of the jungle, wild animals were a part of our daily life. The grunts and snorts of wild pigs often broke the silence of the night. The shrieking of hyenas was frightening, and though we knew them to be far away in the woods, they would sound eerily close, almost as if they were at our door! A couple of times a wild pig got trapped in our orchard, and the guards and the dairy man, Chandan Singh, slaughtered it and had a feast. The ribs were made into a tasty pickle by Mom. Once my grandfather brought home a young deer shot by him on a hunting expedition, and Mom pickled its meat, and shared it with every one, for it was considered to be good to eat it during the cold winters. The deer-skin was made into a cover for a suitcase!

When the monsoon started, the place would be teeming with snakes. There were routine encounters; like once when I went into the bathroom, there was a snake more than two yards long drinking water dripping from the tap. Before I could scream, it quietly slithered away through a hole, swaggering with a perfect 'S'. The following week, my cousin went to get a quilt out at bedtime, and there was a snake curled up on the pile of quilts. He too escaped before she could scream. I say 'escape' as the done thing was to kill any snake that had been spotted. I guess living at the edge of the forest our fear was greater than our compassion.

I spoke to my Uncle about the menace created by the snakes, and he explained to me that it was us humans who had created the menace. When we cut down the forests to build our towns, the animals and birds could quickly relocate to new places in the receding woods, but the sub-terrainian creatures like snakes, toads, rats and many types of worms could not quickly find their way out of the now, uninhabitable terrain. It could take them years to do so, for whenever they ventured out, the changed ecology almost killed them. I remember when it rained, our compound was so full of earthworms that if we needed to step out, we would take along salt, which we sprinkled on them to kill them, and then walked out. That was nature's great vermiculture factory!

One afternoon a cousin came to call me very

conspiratorially, and said, "Come out fast. Its very exciting but don't tell anyone. The gardener just told me that in a corner of the garden, under a huge pile of stones, a female snake has just hatched her eggs, and a lot of tiny snakes have been born." We scampered after her to see the sight, quietly, lest Mom got wind of it. In our innocent childhood we never once wondered what would happen if the snake was to be there! The gardener helped us perch on a rock to see the sight from a distance. There were some seven or eight tiny snakes, slithering and piling on to each other, some greyish tiny crushed eggshells, almost the size of marbles in a heap nearby, but no sign of the mother. The gardener began to shout, "Oh God! She has eaten them up; she has eaten up her own babies! There were more than twenty when they were hatched. Oh God!" We sat around him as he told us that snakes often do this because they are very hungry after sleeping on the eggs for so many days, without venturing out for food. But he added it was good they died. They had been saved from one more rebirth and a wretched reptile's life of a hundred or two hundred years. I silently thought, wouldn't it be great to live for two hundred years, and why is he saying it is good they died, devoured by their own mother—such an unimaginably horrible fate!

Soon a very tragic, and for me devastating incident took place. My cousin Gurcharan, who lived at Jail Road, was sitting in the veranda of her house, cleaning her slate, for we did not have many note books then. Her brother Kulbir was beside her, cutting a dry reed to make a pen for himself, the kind you dip in ink and write with on a wooden slate. She sat with one foot dangling and the other tucked under her buttocks. Suddenly, from the corner of the yard, a black Cobra appeared and came swishing towards her dangling foot; she became still and froze with fear; the Cobra raised its hood and stung her toe. As she screamed, Kulbir bent and saw the snake as it quickly disappeared into the bushes. He immediately held his sister as she was in immense pain. As he had recognized the snake to be a Cobra, he knew it was a dangerous situation. He called out to people who came running, while with the sharp knife he had in his hand, he cut a long slit in Gurcharan's foot where the sting wound was, to make it bleed. It is believed that doing so may help bleed away the snake's poison and prevent it from reaching the vital organs of the victim. Kulbir even sucked the blood from the wound and spat it out many times, but Gurcharan soon fainted. She was rushed to the nearby hospital, but had died within minutes of being stung.

I was very sad when the news was broken to me. I wept and wept. I hated all snakes and wanted them all to be killed. For the first time in my life I felt that pain in my heart, that grief, that sorrow, that loss of a loved one!

I insisted on visiting Gurcharan's house, so after some days Mom took me there. Gurcharan's mother hugged me and everybody sat and talked about her and cried. She said, "You know, we called in a snake-charmer who played his flute and called out the vicious snake which killed her. Even Kulbir recognised it. The snake-charmer said that he spoke to the snake, and it told him that Gurcharan had one night relieved herself over its hole; that was the reason it bit her out of revenge. Cobras are a revered species, being close to God Shiva, and their habit of taking revenge is legendary.

This left me very perturbed! I could not believe it, yet I wanted to believe it, for then it would make sense as to why my innocent little cousin had to die.

Soon it was time for school to re-open, so we returned to Bombay. School was a fifteen minute walk away and lasted all day. My friends were all smart urban kids who talked about cinema, which I had never heard about, and the new styles of filmy dancing! We played cricket and table-tennis, went to the beach on Sundays and made sand castles and collected shells, and ate lots of *Bhel-Puri*. This was exciting, and with studies and homework time just flew. But as the mango blossoms began to appear on the trees, I started longing to be 'home' in Haldwani, to be near my own dear mango trees. Mom told me that the blossoms came early in Bombay because of the difference in the climate, as in Bombay there were no winters. It was decided that I would go to Lucknow with *Bauji's* friend, Gurdit Singh, who was going to hold the marriage ceremony of his son there. *Bauji* was also coming to Lucknow for the wedding, and from there he would take me to Haldwani. Uncle Gurdit had booked a whole coach for the '*baraat*', and there were two cooks who cooked all our meals. Two days and two nights of the journey were so much fun—singing, dancing, joking, pulling each other's leg, and above all eating great freshly cooked food on a moving train.

We stayed in Lucknow and for three days were pampered to a fault by the bride's family. They took us around sightseeing. I will never forget sailing on the Gomti river on huge boats, the trip to the historical '*Bara Imambara*', with its amazing labyrinth, which is said to be connected underground to Fatehpur Sikri in Agra, and a special trip to the '*Hazrat Ganj*' market for the best savouries in North India, like '*Papri Chaat*' and '*Dahi Bhalla*'. Not to forget the festive meals where they served quail and pheasant for dinner, besides the famous Lucknow '*kebabs*', and rich desserts. The only other trip I enjoyed so much was to Asansol later when I was fourteen years old, to attend the marriage of my cousin 'Honey', whose foster mother was the Inspector of Mines there, and who organized a full day's trip inside an operative coal mine, an experience that I'll never forget. Later when we saw an Amitabh Bacchan movie called, '*Kala Patthar*', I could remember the visit and tell my kids that I had been inside a coal mine and actually seen the blasting and collecting of coals, and the miserable poor workers, who were not even allowed the dignity to walk out freely after work for they were searched, lest they be taking away small bits of coal!

After three days, *Bauji* and I left for Haldwani. It was great to be home with my friends and cousins, and Trilochan uncle's son Amarjit, whom I love as much as my brother, Gullu, even now. Summer nights we invariably slept outdoors, for we believed in the Easterlies—a band of fairies who came to soothe and caress you to sleep; indoors you would miss them! My aunt Kuljeet and *Mataji*, my grandmother slept under the porch with Amarjit sleeping beside her. *Bauji* slept indoors.

One night, horror of horrors, something thick and long fell across *Mataji*'s bed from the roof of the porch and she woke up startled. But the most terrible shock came when the thing moved, and she knew at once that it was a snake. In a swift and powerful reaction, she pushed it with all her strength and it fell to the ground. The poor snake must have got a shock too, first falling from the roof and then being thrown off the bed! As she softly awoke aunty, so as not to startle her, the snake crawled away towards the house door where *Buaji*, my grandfather's sister was sleeping in the smaller veranda, and remained there. Aunty awoke uncle who awoke *Buaji*, which was important for only she had the guts to awaken *Bauji*, and only *Bauji* knew how to kill a snake. That was done and the poor rattled snake was killed with one blow of a thick stick. I slept through the whole 'drama'. Next morning when I was told about it, I was cross with everyone for making me miss all the excitement.

Later whenever *Mataji* would talk about this episode to people, she always said, "It is so surprising that the snake did not move at all after stopping outside the door, for it did take some time to awaken *Bauji* and for him to be composed and find the stick." And everyone said, "It is all destiny. Its death brought it here." But I still shudder to think of worse possibilities and thank God that we all came out of it safe and sound.

Many years passed by, growing up, developing new interests, reading, college, and then I married. We were in Haldwani once again in the early eighties. *Bauji* was no more and daddy had let out his part of the house to the WHO, the part where Mrs Tiku used to live, and they had started a Malaria Research centre in it. They had built fish tanks in the courtyard, where they bred different types of tiny fish that fed on mosquito larvae, giving them a natural and non-chemical way of dealing with the problem of Malaria, a killer disease in those parts. The Doctor in charge of the Centre had a strange hobby—he collected snakes. He would pick up different types of species, observe them for some days, and then leave them back in the wilderness. His wife told me that when she had come as a bride, she had been shocked to see a snake in the cupboard, and when she screamed, the Doctor said, "Oh that one? Don't worry its mine." She had literally fainted on being subsequently he told that he had twenty seven of them in the house!

On this trip my kids were with me, the older two Chingi and Ricky grown up enough to climb trees. One day the doctor called us to his lab and announced that for the first time in his life, he had caught a black Cobra, live, and would get it out the next day to feed it, for snakes eat once in two or three days, and we could all come and watch it eating while the doctor made a film of the event. We went next evening. The cobra was brought out and put in one of the dry fish tanks. A small water snake was put for its dinner. But Mr Cobra was not interested. It spread its hood and put out its fangs menacingly but simply ignored the tiny snake. After an hour the water snake was taken away and the cobra went back to the lab. Next day, out of curiosity, we went again. Everyone was crowded around the lab table, and we were told that as they had fed the Cobra a mouse, it had swallowed it up whole, and immediately its abdomen had burst, killing it at once. We looked, and it was such a ghastly sight, the bleeding black Cobra, the mouse stuck between the flesh, and tiny insects, parasites that had lived in its stomach, crawling out of the wound, like mice from a sinking ship. Ugh it was horrible!

Chapter 9

Sophia College Bombay

In the Fifties our business in Bombay was flourishing by leaps and bounds. In the year 1958, my third sister, 'Pappu' was born, bringing happiness to my parents. She became the darling of the neighbourhood. We had an Ambassador car now, and Daddy would take us out every week, mostly to town for lunch at a good restaurant. At that time Bombay was under 'prohibition', which meant that you could not buy or sell liquor or even drink it. Daddy had taken a special permit to buy two bottles of liquor in a month, one of which had to be brandy for I would need it often. In fact, I was already quite fond of brandy and on days when I played a lot and my legs pained, or if I had a cold, I would ask Dadddy for a spoon full of brandy. I loved the warmth and relaxation I felt on drinking it, though Mummy was not in favour of it. In 1960, Niku, my youngest sister was born. She was, I think, born a sage, wise and sensitive, with a very soft and caring nature. She was easily *Bauji's* favourite. By 1960, Daddy had not only sent lots of money to Haldwani, to widen our business activities there, he had also bought three bungalows in Khar in Bombay! One was on the Linking Road — a huge bungalow with a drive and a porch, and a big double storey annexe. Built in the Parsi style, it was very beautiful. But we lived in a slightly smaller house half a mile from the Khar station. This one we had bought from a Parsi gentleman, Mr Ginwalla. It was a single storey house with huge rooms and a lovely semi-circular balcony. It had some exotic plants growing—there was a *'supari'* tree, a *chickoo* tree, and even some pineapples growing in the back-yard, along with the regular coconut palms and mango trees. The lawn on one side had very pretty evergreens all around and there were flowers of all colours and a Gujarati style *'Jhoola'* a large swing, in a shady patch on the right side of the house. I really enjoyed living in this house. Later, we also bought the house adjoining this one, a large one built on 1100 sq yards of land. It had small apartments all fully rented out. We were able to join together the compounds of both houses, giving us a very big vacant plot in between the two houses, something very rare in Bombay. All the functions for my wedding were organised here. After that the Communist Party in Bombay kept using it for their meetings with Daddy's approval.

There is an interesting episode about the people from whom we acquired the new house. They lived in the house opposite ours, and we soon began to see a lot of them for they had a telephone connection, which we did not. At that time if one needed to make an outstation call, one had to book a 'trunk call', as they called it, through the telephone exchange, and wait for one's turn to be connected, sometimes a couple of hours! As our family was spread between Haldwani, Nainital and Bombay, we needed to talk often on the phone, and those days, neighbours with phones were usually very co-operative. These were a middle aged couple (middle age half a century back would begin at thirty five years; my own Mom was just thirty five when I got married!), with a daughter who had just joined college. If we got a call or one that we had booked matured, they would call us at once, and we were grateful. The gentleman did not go to work, and the lady was rarely seen, except some evenings when she would come out for a walk, but when we went to their house to take the calls, they were very warm and hospitable. The lady was very beautiful and charming with immaculate manners. She spoke perfect Hindi with a smattering of Urdu, in a soft musical voice. However some other neighbours kept warning us that they were not good people; in fact they said that she actually was a professional 'gentlemen's lady consort'. They pointed out the luxurious cars parked outside her house at night till the early hours of the morning. But we always found her in simple clothes, her *sari pallu* always covering her head, and a large '*bindi*' on her forehead. Whatever it was, gradually our visits to their house became more frequent, for when *Bauji* learnt that the house adjoining ours belonged to them, he started negotiating a deal with them to buy it. Some months went by till the deal was finalised and some more while *Bauji* arranged for the money. Meanwhile, Asha their daughter, and I had become very friendly. We'd chat every evening before dinner for a while. She told me she had a boy friend whom she wanted to marry, but his parents were not allowing it. One day when I felt bold enough, I asked her to show me her mother's room upstairs, for I had heard that it was very beautifully done up, with ethnic furniture and lovely lamps, and even had a *sitar* and *tablas*. She agreed. The next time when her mother went to the Shiva temple with her father, she called me and took me upstairs. The room did not belong to a middle class household; it was straight out of a palace! The upholstery, the curtains, exotic cushions and long puffed up bolsters, all were in pure silk, very soft and beautiful. There was also a '*Hookah*', and the best wine glasses on the sideboard. Wow! The carpet was of the softest Cahmere wool too!

Then she told me that her mother's profession was to entertain gentlemen of high breeding and cultural backgrounds. They came here to unwind, in peace, to get what they did not get elsewhere; some special '*raga*' that they wanted to hear, not at a performance but from a singer who sang only for them. They wanted an intelligent companion. When they wished to discuss business or even family problems, she would give them an understanding audience while they poured their problems out, quietly offer a drink, and listen some more. She never offered suggestions or solutions, only let them talk, at their pace. Some men just wanted homely comfort away from home, and she provided that. She had been trained from childhood in traditional classic music and dance, having descended from a family of royal courtesans, who were never called 'women of pleasure', but were respectfully called '*Baiji*'. Men came and spent several hours in the company of this talented, educated, cultured lady. I wanted to ask Asha, if she slept with her 'friends', as Asha called them, but restrained myself. She whispered to me in a moment of magnanimity, that these men left anything from five thousand to ten thousand rupees. Wow! Promising not to talk about this to anyone, I came back home, my mind and my heart in a turmoil, writhing with conflicting and confusing emotions; but I did feel I should respect her more for she was helping so many men, maybe preventing so many homes from breaking up, and many men from cracking up! I had seen Daddy confused and upset whenever an issue came up regarding *Bauji*, Trilochan Uncle, or *Mataji*, and Mummy could not help him for she herself was biased; I could understand the comfort this lady would be offering to her friends, or so I thought at that time.

In 1964 my youngest sibling, 'Gullu', was born, in answer to everyone's prayers, almost like a miracle. Mummy was not keeping well, as she had asthma, for which there were only steroids, which were debilitating in their own way. So when it was known that Mummy was pregnant, *Bauji* decided that she should not live in polluted Bombay, but shift to Nainital for her delivery. The pure air would help fight asthma, and she would be more relaxed and healthy. So Dad, Mummy, my two sisters, shifted to Nainital, and I stayed on in Bombay with *Mataji* and *Bauji*. When Mummy was in the seventh month of pregnancy, she was shifted to the hospital where *Bauji* arranged two rooms for Mummy's comfort. *Mataji* also went to stay with her in the hospital, for the rest of the pregnancy. They had decided that whether it was a girl or a boy, Mummy would be operated for tubectomy, so she would not go through any more pregnancies. God was kind to us and on the 13th of November, 1964, he gifted us Gullu, my baby brother. The religious ceremonies held and pilgrimages undertaken to thank the Lord were countless. The day the news of the birth came, I saw *Bauji* crying for the first time. Gullu's birth brought so much joy and relief to the family.

During Mummy's long absence, I had begun to stay

weekends with my *Nanaji's* family, who had also shifted to Bombay, and now that all my mother's brothers were married and there were children in that house, I enjoyed myself thoroughly. My uncles led very colourful lives, and loved taking me with them, to 'flaunt' their smart and knowledgeable English speaking niece among their friends. All restaurants those days had a dance floor, and throughout the evening couples would enjoy dancing, eating, drinking and again dancing. I got to see different types of ballroom dances, and saw women dancing with different partners, unlike at home where women hardly even spoke to men outside the family. One Sunday afternoon my Moni uncle took me to a "Jam Session" at a new restaurant. The experience was fabulous; it was an afternoon of rock-n-roll, very smart and energetic dancers took part, the short dresses of the ladies swirling around their legs, even flying in the air, and couples taking turns to rest in between the numbers, choosing better and better partners, until finally one couple was left dancing alone. They finished their flurry of swift steps in each others' arms with a spontaneous kiss, to everyone's delight! It was such a beautiful gesture!

I enjoyed going for night shows of English movies with my uncles. They also enjoyed with me for their wives had no interest in English movies. I not only enjoyed them but had no qualms discussing the films with them too while munching a hotdog with a coke at midnight. Most weekend evenings though we spent at the Cricket Club of India, the CCI across Churchgate, for my uncles were, and still are, compulsive gamblers. Their day is not complete without a session of cards. Though I did not play with money, I hung around, and admired the elderly Parsi ladies, in their gorgeous saris and immaculate shoes, who sat till the wee hours playing cards. I remember one particular old lady who needed a magnifying glass to see her cards, but with what gusto, she enjoyed life and kept herself happy. Years later when I was in college, Moni *Mamaji* took me to the Mahalaxmi Race Course to witness the Derby, a special race where the best horses and jockeys take part and the stakes are outrageously high. The thrill pervading the whole course, the well-dressed people, horse owners, everyone was euphoric, everyone seemed to be sure of making a killing. The races began in the midst of loads of bonhomie with everyone saying to each other, "Oh Wow! You've come, it's great. We'll have fun, and all the best!" but as the races began, they were all for themselves—what mattered was their own bets, and their signals to their bookies. I wondered if there was any real difference between the smallest and the biggest better, and why did some people spend a fortune to dress for the occasion, but *Mamaji* told me it was like a ritual—the sunglasses, the hats, the slim fair young ladies on the side, cheering wildly! I realized that though they were perspiring through their designer dresses, they wanted to keep alive their image of 'nonchalant race fans'. During the race, everyone just cheered their favourite horses; such a frenzy pervaded the atmosphere with everyone calling out to their chosen horses, the jockeys, and within their hearts, to their Gods to help them win! When the race ended, some people cheered, and some just plumbed into despair. I saw people picking up their winnings with great glee, and as we were leaving I heard an old bookie saying, "huh! Let them splurge now, but the money's all going to come back right here, that's the golden rule!"

During this time I made many friends, read all that I could, studied hard, and consolidated my childhood ambition of joining the medical profession. I worked hard and did everything that would help me get admission in the medical college. I scored very well in the school leaving examination.Now I needed to get into a good college for a year of pre-medical studies, which would make me eligible for the medical college. It had been made quite clear to me that I would only be allowed to go to a girls' college, so I had decided to join Sophia College.

After being congratulated for my result and the event duly celebrated and rewarded by everyone, the day for the admission to the college arrived. Daddy came with me, and that hour in the cab became the most crucial of my life, wherein my happy carefree life was turned upside down, and all my wishes turned to dust. During that cab journey, Daddy started to convince me against taking the medical subjects. "They are too tough", he said. I'd never get to enjoy college, and it would take me so many years to actually become a doctor. "But Daddy, this is all I have ever wanted to do. I have never thought of doing anything else, I can't think of doing anything else. If I don't get to be a doctor, then there's no point in my life any more. You remember Daddy, even as a child, I used to be learning to give injections, using pumpkins and aubergines, and be chasing the doctors to teach me more. And they would tell me that I must study medicine when I grow up. I'll work harder than ever, Daddy; please don't take away my dream from me." Even now while writing this, my eyes burn with tears. I remember how my childhood dreams were shattered and for the first time in my life I was denied anything. I was being denied life itself. My heart broke. And that part still remains broken. Daddy said, "Actually *Bauji* wants to fix your engagement soon. He wants to see you married to a good boy from a good family, and so do your mother and I." But poor Daddy was too honest to manipulate me, and he hid his face and wept when he said. "Nothing we say or do will make a difference; what *Bauji* wants only will be done, so you better change your mind. Its better you take 'Humanities', and enjoy college for some time; you will not be able to complete your graduation as people are after us with proposals for you and we'll be getting you engaged soon."

That was that. I was 14 years old, and my heart was broken forever. After that episode life was a duty to be fulfilled, never my life any more. From then on I lived only to be a good daughter, a good wife, a good daughter-in-law and a good mother; a good mother-in law, a good grandmother, a good cook, a good teacher, a good tailor, a good nurse, a good business-woman, a good adviser, a good financial-balancer, and whatever else. I could not forgive Daddy for what he did to me for a very long time. I believed he should have stood by me, but I realised that despite the high learning and lofty ideals, both my parents were also eager to see me married. So after that, life became only a "destiny"!

I wondered how my mother sat by and let my only aim in life be burst like a bubble! She was always the 'militant' one; Daddy was too reticent and docile. She had never taken anything lying down; she would fight with clenched teeth if she felt something was not right. I had seen her argue with *Bauji* despite her '*purdah*', and also *Mataji*. When her brother, my Rajinder *Mamaji* left Daddy's company, and there was a quarrel over the amount of money due to him by our family, she stood by her brother and fought with Daddy. She even took out the Partnership Deed that had been signed by both *Mamaji* and Daddy, and which was the only proof that Daddy could show anyone who would arbitrate in the matter, and left it at her brother's house, so Daddy could not assert himself. This hurt Daddy till his last days. He would often tell me, "after that happened, I lost all respect in *Bauji's* eyes; I could never face him again".

So where was all that 'fight for the right is what Guru Gobind Singhji has taught us, his true Sikhs,' when her own daughter was being scarified? Mummy had always been like her name, *Daler*, the brave one. She had told me how in Iran where she lived as a child, the method of slaughtering goats and chicken was *'Halal'*, the Muslim way. This is not allowed for the Sikhs. We kill the animal with one stroke of the butcher's knife on its neck, a quick stroke so as to kill it quickly. She had learnt to do that from the servants. She was so brave, she could kill a goat or a sheep with one stroke of the knife, hacking the neck away from the body. But she would not fight for me. She always regaled me with stories of her ancestors' being bold and pioneering people. Her grandfather had set out from his village of 'Mundee' near Rawalpindi, to search for a land route to Iran, to be able to trade with that country, in the 19th century. Treading over hills and plains, the rough terrain of Afghanistan, using horses and mules, even camels or on foot, he had returned after 9 years, with loads of wealth. So on his next journey, he took along several young men from his village and neighbouring areas to try their fortunes abroad, and with God's grace, they all became rich traders. Mummy's father, whom we called *'Pitaji'*, was friendly with the Shah of Iran, and had earned the contracts for building the barracks and other defence installations for the Iranian army.

It is amazing how adventurous and pioneering my great-grandfather was and how fearless. He is said to have travelled to Samarkand and Russia, and we still have at home a relic of his sojourns, a Russian '*Samovar*' which is used to make tea, and a mention of which is found in works of Russian writers. My grandfather told me that he had done trade with China, selling Persian carpets to the Chinese, and bringing Chinese silks to India, which included Pakistan then. He mentioned once there was a temporary ban on the export of silk, but they managed to 'smuggle' out the fabric, paying for it in opium and in gold coins. And we believe that scams are happening only now!

Later *Pitaji* did the same work in India in Dehradun, but unfortunately lost all the wealth earned over half a century in some bad ventures with the Indian government. While studying in Dehradun, Mummy learnt to shoot guns and even rifles, which an average woman could not even carry. She had so much faith in Guruji, that no amount of suffering could shake it. She believed that Guruji had filled us Sikhs with an unusual power, and we were never to be afraid. Once as a teenager she was in her village when they came to know that dacoits were coming to their village to plunder. There were a few families in the village, but no men folk were at home, of which the dacoits were aware. Normally there was great fear of the Sikhs all around, and robbers avoided places where there were Sikhs. So Mummy called a few friends, and also a couple of young lads, and they all put on turbans like the men, dressed in manly clothes, with *Kirpaans* hanging from their shoulders, and the long *Kirpaans* held in their hands, and went and sat in the Gurudwara. It seems that the robbers came and peeped into the Gurudwara, and said, "we have been misinformed, the Sikh men are very much there and sitting in the Gurudwara. Let us run away before we are killed." I never stopped marvelling at her bravery. But where was it now, when her child needed it?

Strangely, I never even lamented to her about my disappointment. She was happy with her children enjoying bringing them up. She must have missed that with me, with *Bauji, Mataji* having taken me over completely; I even slept with *Mataji* and not with Mummy! I don't think it mattered to her what I did, as long as I was married off well, and happily. That's what she often told me.

And these were the people with whom I had grown up to be *ME*, the way I think, and the way *I AM*. With their upbringing I cultivated, a strong character, confidence, a thinking mind, my values, my standards, my beliefs, even independence of thought ! I began to recognize hypocrisy as a way of life, and not just a one- time tactic to tide over a situation. Every one is a hypocrite, with no exceptions. Those who trumpet their integrity are also hypocrites. So there!

The U-turn had happened, I filled the form for a course

in 'Arts', got admission in Sophia's College, and learnt to make the best of things. The childhood grooming of doing my best and working hard helped me in doing well throughout college. In the very first year I made a mark as a good student, I read voraciously, finishing a book almost every day. I would read all the reference books possible. I took part in several cultural activities, debates, theatre, and even joined music classes to learn to play the '*Tabla*'! The First Year Arts results were extraordinarily rewarding, for I passed with a First Division, one of only eight students in Bombay who got a First Division. I was in Nainital enjoying my summer holidays when the result arrived. Rory, my friend from Delhi was there too. *Bauji* was in Haldwani and Daddy sent him a telegram to give him the good news. He was elated and though it was late evening, he left for Nainital to personally congratulate me. He reached at 9 pm and Rory and I were not even at home; we had persuaded aunty to allow us to go and enjoy the romance of boating at night, under the starry sky, and she almost fainted when *Bauji* asked for me. He wouldn't tell her why he had come so late, and she kept making excuses about me helping the neighbour's kid with maths! We rowed the boat across the windy lake, singing songs, till the boatman had to turn in the boat for all the boats were counted at night. We reached home giggling at ten o'clock. When we entered, aunty tried to quickly tell us about the kid with maths problems but before she could

I had told *Bauji* we had gone boating. Either he was very happy with my result, or knew when not to spoil a good thing, he simply got out the telegram and the whole house burst into celebration.

Rory and I decided to celebrate in a special way on the last day of our holiday, when we would leave Haldwani for Delhi, I to join college in Bombay and she hers in Delhi. Often with Trilochan uncle, when he stopped at 'B Das & Co' in Tallital Bazaar to browse among the liquors, while he spent time selecting his gin and beer, whiskey and rum, I would browse too and discovered Apple Cider that contained two percent alcohol. I asked uncle if I could have it, and from then on he would get me a bottle of cider often. On the day we were to travel, we stole a bottle of beer from Uncle's bar, chilled it in the freezer, and sat in a corner room, sipping it in tall glasses, munching cheese cubes and salted cashew nuts—the thrill of our first beer and the fear of getting caught mingling into a delightful mood, which we both still remember fondly.

During the First year I was engaged to be married. One Sunday Mummy said to me, "Your Daddy and I have seen a boy for you and we like him." I retorted, "you go marry him then!" At this Mummy got wild and said that I was disrespectful. I shrugged, and let the episode pass. But they were serious. Two weeks later, one morning Mummy told me that I was not to go to college, as I was to be formally betrothed, and my 'fiancé –to-be' and his family were coming over in the evening for the '*Ardaas*' or solemnising ceremony. I found it very funny. I rang up my friends and gave them the 'news' and they laughed with me. They all believed it was a prank I was playing. I told them to come over in the evening. I felt no involvement in whatever was going on, I never asked who the people were, my fiancé's name, nothing. It was totally unreal, as if it was happening to someone else. It couldn't be me! I was only 14, and felt no interest; I had no feelings for the opposite sex. I had wrapped myself in academic pursuits. I loved to read and discuss business and politics. I abhorred womanly weaknesses. Thoughts had to be logical, not emotional, and also the conversation.

But there it was, I was actually getting engaged. My friends asked mummy my fiancé's name and she said, 'Balbir'. They asked if we would be meeting him, and she said 'No', but we could peep from the window when they came, and described him somewhat. My friends and I were having fun and laughing as though we were at a Hindi Movie. Eleven men came for the engagement, no women. We girls took position at the bedroom window, with even a camera ready to 'shoot' the guy. After the older men had entered, there were four young guys, all beaming away and blushing—all four looked eligible. With the cursory look we got of them, we guessed it could be the taller man with the shiny turban, and left it at that. I never asked anyone which was the man I was getting engaged to, it didn't matter! Though I did wonder how I would recognize him, when I found four young men looking so much alike. I could only differentiate between them by observing the colour of their turbans!

Much later we came to know that the tall guy was Balbir's elder brother.

Six months later, a dinner was held for my 'in-laws', when my mother-in law came over for the first time. She gave me a set of gold jewellery, and made me wear it, but was disappointed that I could not wear the earrings for my ears had not been pierced! That night also Balbir was brought in for a moment so that we could 'see' each other. Well, in all the commotion, I didn't see much, he could have been any other sikh of his age and build; I don't know what Balbir saw. He gave me a silly looking ring, and rushed out before I could see it. That is the record of our first meeting, and I'm writing this after almost 45 years!

College was the best thing that happened to me, in my short life pre-marriage. It was the first time I went out of the house unchaperoned by my very militant maid, 'Sonabai', who was my shadow and constant companion. Travelling by the Bombay local trains has a thrill of its own. We would catch the 8.10 or 8.12 'fast' from Khar station to Churchgate, get off at Grant Road, and then either walk or share a cab. We soon formed a close group of friends. Some came from Santa-Cruz, I joined at Khar, but we always waited for each other to be on the same train. Soon we became like veterans, travelling on the foot-boards, jumping out at every station and jumping on again, having lots of fun. We'd try to beat each other to jump from the running train, grab a '*nimboo-paani*', drain the glass and run to catch the same train as it shot out of the station, all in the twenty seconds that the train stopped at 'Dadar'! Returning from college we often took a bus, and those bus journeys are unforgettable, sitting on the top floor of the red BEST double decker bus, in the first row, enjoying the breeze smelling of salt and sand, watching the huge waves of the Arabian Sea while crossing Mahalaxmi and Worli. During the monsoons, the high tide threw the waves right up to our windows, on the upper deck!

Even in college we created a cult of our own and were known as Fatty's gang, Fatty being me! We were bold, snooty, very mischievous, and very brainy and all toppers. Once when the authorities put a notice outside the staff-room saying, "Students are not to enter the staff-room", we added to it, "except when the male staff is alone!" It created a ruckus in the girls' college, till the Economics professor, Mr Tyrewalla guessed it was me. We provoked, scandalised, even made fun of some of the teachers, but we also gave them respect and good results. In our second year we were visited by Mr. Jayprakash Narain, the old Gandhian leader, who requested us to work for people affected by the massive floods in Bihar. So we formed the 'Bihar Flood Relief

Committee' to collect funds. After college, we went door to door, asking for old clothes or money, and if people gave neither, we'd request them to give us their old newspapers, which nobody denied. That was our level of perseverance and commitment! In fact, one evening we were near Balbir's house and as he was passing by, he was shocked to see us lugging newspapers, for by now we had met a couple of times. I nonchalantly asked him to take them in his car and deliver them at our college the next day. We also organised an evening of variety entertainment in our college auditorium, where we had the famous Hindi Poet 'Qamar Jalalabadi' as chief guest. The proceeds of the sale of tickets went to the Bihar Relief Fund. Most of my teachers were fond of me. They said they loved to hear me speak '*shudh*' Hindi. I was quite uninhibited and witty, and enjoyed long conversations with many of my teachers. It must have been difficult for the young male teachers to be surrounded by so many good looking girls everyday. When Balbir came to the college to drop the old newspapers, I was pleasantly surprised when two of my professors gracefully took it upon themselves to entertain him to tea in the canteen. They became my friends after that and I would often share my concerns with them, for with my friends I kept up a 'macho', 'devil may care' image. All the eighteen teachers from Sophia College attended my wedding, and one of them even took the trouble to visit us while on a trip to Delhi, to convince Balbir to let me finish my graduation. I continued to visit the college and meet them all.

'SUPW' as the schools call it now, was being experimented with, to make it a part of regular education programmes, and our college was one of the pioneers in this work. Later our college adopted tribal village called Kosbad near 'Dahanu Road' a small town on the border of Maharashtra and Gujarat. We volunteers would travel from Bombay by train, and the BDO of the village would take us there in his jeep. We would be there from Saturday evening to Monday morning, and work with the 'Adivasis' who were a part of the 'Waarli' tribe.

This village was the most idyllic place I had seen. Tiny green hillsides sloping down to the Arabian Sea, small bays and smaller beaches, lush paddy fields! We fell in love with it. Only when we had a meeting at night with the social workers there, that we came to know the real plight of the villagers. They grew only rice, and knew no other farming. They ate only rice—they had no vegetables or pulses for their meals; occasionally they would get some tamarinds and have them soaked in water with their rice. The per-capita consumption of edible oil per family was only half a litre in a year! A School had just been started by the government, but only boys were sent to school, and that too so that they would be able to go to the cities and get work there.

At first sight, their lives seemed to be quite barren; the

barest of food, the barest of clothes—unmarried girls wore no blouses, they simply wrapped their scanty saris around their shoulders; few boys wore shirts, most were in knickers; their huts had nothing in the name of furniture, the area was expanses of green fields with brown patches of clearing for the huts. It is interesting to note that even the most frugal hut had a colourful '*Rangoli*' design at the door, beautifully drawn by hand, using coloured clay. But after they retired from the fields, and after the frugal meals, for even we were given '*Jowar roties*' (simple *chapattis* made of '*jowar*'a cheap cereal) with *chutney*, the whole population of the village would get together to celebrate. We got to witness the rich 'Waarli' culture when everyone sang together in their particular dialect, to the tune of a unique trumpet-like instrument made of dried gourds! They invited us to dance with them, which we did, in order to gain their friendship. We would make a huge semi-circle together, arms entwined with each other in perfect unison, taking two steps right and one step left in a very fast rhythm. Everyone had to be perfectly tuned or we'd either step on each others feet, or get our own feet trampled. It was almost like a trance! Men and women danced together, and the bare backs of the young girls blended perfectly with the scene, with the women getting the respect they should. No, we saw no chauvinism there! By midnight, people would leave for their homes, tired and happy. We enjoyed ourselves too.

We wanted to teach them the use of fertilizers, but they would not allow us, for fear of us releasing evil 'spirits' upon their fields by spraying 'magic powders'! We tricked them by spraying one half of some of the fields with fertilizer in the night while they were asleep. When we returned the following fortnight, we explained to them why one half of the paddy had grown taller, and then they believed us. Once the head-man of the village was convinced, everyone followed, and soon all the fields were giving better crop. We also planted a 'drumstick' tree in each house. This is a highly popular vegetable on the west coast, also very nutritious, and the plant needs hardly any care. We were teaching them to get better nourishment, and to use vegetables and fruits in their diet.

In an interesting incident, my eldest son 'Chingi' got his name when I was in that village. On one of the trips, I was doing a skit in Marathi, during the entertainment time in the night, using a doll as a baby girl, I being her mother, and fantasising about her bright future—a very comic skit which had the whole gathering in splits, especially since I, a city girl was performing; and the baby's name was, 'Chingi'! So when I got married the following year, my friends began teasing me, saying, "When is 'Chingi' arriving"? And so when my son was born, he was automatically named, 'Chingi'.

Things were not good in India. The 1962 war with China had seen our first Prime Minister crushed and left the country dumbfounded, but rising united to fight at all levels, sending a wave of patriotism across the land. But the 1965 war with Pakistan left us shattered. It lasted two weeks, and our brave Prime Minister who negotiated the cease-fire in Russia, died mysteriously. The losses of the war and several natural calamities left hunger and strife everywhere. When we worked in Kosbad, we got no sugar in our tea, it was that dear! India lost much respect internationally, and suffered the ignominy of the P L 480 food grains, donated to us by the United States. They were poor quality grains but gratefully accepted by a hungry country. In college we could not bear the shame of PL480, and could not forget it easily; even today and it is a most hurtful memory. The much nurtured Trade Union Movement ended up killing the industry; most mills were shut down, silencing the 9 o'clock and 5 o'clock sirens, and thousands and thousands of workers rendered jobless, facing famished families; thousands of them turning to crime too.

Meanwhile Balbir had asked permission from Mummy to meet me sometimes, and I decided to meet him at Juhu, near the Gandhi statue, and after that we could have coffee at the Juhu Hotel. I took along my gang of seven girls with me, and stuck to them all afternoon, I did not know what to say or do without them, and Balbir was awfully peeved, but went along. On that date I think he actually enjoyed being with so many smart girls, and treating us all to high tea. He was highly impressed when we spoke to each other in French! But after a couple of times, having to lug around seven girls when he wanted to meet me, began to upset him, and he told me to meet him alone at Metro for a movie. I bunked college and went. It was a Rock Hudson and Doris Day comedy called "Send Me No Flowers". I really enjoyed it, but afterwards in the lift when Balbir tried to kiss me, I felt brutally assaulted and pushed him away violently, which made him very angry. He stopped calling me up. But in a few days, I think he must have missed me and my chatter, for he called up again, but I said I would not go for a movie and suggested we sit in the Sea Lounge at the Taj, for there one could sit as long as one liked with a minimum order of a cup of tea. The huge windows gave a stunning view of the sea, lined with ships, particularly at sunset. He kept trying to convince me that a couple engaged to be married ought to kiss each other, but I found it repulsive, though I did not tell him that. I simply said that we would try it another time.

By the end of my second year in college, my wedding date was fixed. Balbir's whole family had come over for dinner, a huge affair organised at home, Mummy making the choicest dishes—Irani chicken, Chinese chicken-livers, fish, and several desserts. I was waiting for it all to end, for I wanted plenty of chicken to be left over, so I could take it along on the next day's trip to Kosbad to treat my friends. After the party, Mummy told me, "We have fixed the date

for your wedding; it is to be on the 21st of Jan next year."
And I said, "Please, pack the left-over chicken in a large box
for tomorrow and also some 30 to 40 'Rasgullas', I will take
them for my friends in Kosbad". The importance of what
she was saying did not sink in, and anyway January was still
far away. I was enjoying myself meanwhile.

But very soon it did start to sink in, and sink in very
hard! Balbir objected to my social work in Kosbad, and
also the Literacy classes in the college. I was shocked! What
harm was there in either? We were only trying to do some
good! But that was it. I never went to Kosbad after that.
I stopped enjoying college also. Still I studied hard. If in
the first year, History had me enraptured, this year it was
Literature. And good old P.G. Woodehouse was our constant
companion. I told myself, whatever else happens, at least my
studies are there, and education will take me to a better life.
I continued to go to college till the 17th of January, 1968,
ready to rejoin after a week, when the wedding ceremonies
would be over, but sadly that was not to be. Another shock!
On the day we got married, Balbir told me he would not
allow me to study any more, and I should forget all about
college and graduation. I swallowed it all, the injury, the
insult, the humility, the helplessness, the futility, all! I never
felt so small in my life.

I never even thought of talking to my parents about it,
for the ritual refrain was, "now that is your house, you have

to do whatever they say, etc."

Religion has always been an important part of my existence. From as early as I can remember, prayer, pious behaviour, good social and human values, were important for the family, also great pride in being a Sikh. We had a large room where the 'Guru Granth Sahib' was worshipped. every morning. *Mataji* would recite the "Sukhmani Sahib", loudly for two hours, and people would congregate to our house, for Haldwani still did not have a proper 'Gurudwara'. The last two verses were recited together by everyone, and it was to that sound that I would wake up! I thank my grandmother for cultivating in me the discipline of reading the religious texts and reciting the verses in music. She has been a very important influence in my life and I was closer to her than my Mom. *Mataji* was a mix of the modern and the orthodox, and I think she made the best use of both to get what she wanted. She was fiercely independent in her thinking, did not argue, but would stick to her own convictions. She would talk of the times when she had gone canvassing for votes for the Congress party, for Govind Ballabh Pant in particular. She would dress smartly and travel in her car with a maid accompanying her. At that time only income-tax payers and their wives could vote for the parliament, so I could imagine the class of people she was approaching for votes! People were wary of letting their wives come out in the open to exercise their franchise, and her main task was to convince them to allow the women to vote. Then she spoke of the times when a live band played on the Flats in Nainital, and English men and women came in their evening dresses and there was ballroom dancing there. Drinks were served freely. She had picked up the habit of being very well dressed from them, for *Bauji* also had good taste. She wore silks from Kashmir, Iran and Sweden, '*Dupattas*' from France; always sparkling white clothes, with medium heeled white court shoes. And she had silver hair; what a personality she had, despite her small height. She massaged her face with 'Hazeline Snow' twice a day, and had a glowing complexion; she taught me never to grimace at anything or anyone, to avoid getting ugly lines across my face! There is a cute incident much later when her nieces were showing her a new beauty product now available in India, the 'Anne French Cleansing Milk' for the face. After her niece explained how one dab of it on cotton wool, rubbed on the face cleaned the face to perfection. *Mataji* asked her to get a bottle for her. When her niece teased her for going in for such products at her age, *Mataji* said, "but I want to use it for my shoes, I like them to be sparkling white!"

She could be quite crafty too. After *Bauji's* death, she lived all alone in Haldwani for several years. She had let out one of the bungalows to a Sales Tax inspector who tormented her by not paying the rent, and instead imposed

Sales-Tax penalties whenever she demanded the rent. After some months, one day, she took some men from the petrol pump, along with a relative of hers to the inspector's house, and all of them began taking measurements of the rooms, the veranda and the boundary wall, with *Mataji* taking notes, very seriously. After she left, the inspector out of curiosity, asked her men what was happening and they told him, "*Mataji* is selling this house to her relative. She is old and alone, she cannot chase you for the rent all the time. Her relative will get this place vacated, for he will want to live here." The inspector, all flustered, came to his senses, and never troubled *Mataji* with the rent again!

As I grew up, I learnt '*Gurmukhi*' the language of our scriptures, and I could also read from the '*Guru Granth Sahib*'. My father told me to read about all religions, and among his books were, the '*Bhagwad Gita*', the '*Hanuman Chalisa*', even the Bible. I read them and imbibed them into my thinking and beliefs. Being in a Catholic school, I also came under Catholic influence, for which I am grateful forever. Without it I may not have learnt the values of patience, fortitude, sympathy, charity, and above all, politeness. Courage and the quality of sharing, my Mom actually drilled into me. She taught me to take the responsiblity for what I did, to never be afraid of anyone, and make faith my main crutch. 'Bow your head only before God, never to any human being,' was Mummy's dictat. She was not only named 'fearless'; she actually was fearless!

A transformation came when I was in class IX. For the first time my friends and I planned to go for a movie by ourselves. The planning was fine, but getting permission from the parents was difficult. Mom had always tantalized me with tales of her freedom when she was a student, her owning a bicycle, and with it the independence to go and come as she fancied, so I thought she would welcome my attempt at some freedom. But no. She said it was not possible here, for *Bauji* was too strict. So all I did that Thursday was sit and sulk, Thursday used to be our mid-week holiday. *Mataji* tried to console me. In the afternoon, she was going for her weekly 'satsang', and she offered to take me along. But I sulked. Then she said, "Come with me,Satvir, and I promise you one thing, if by the end of the 'satsang', you even once remember that your friends are at the movie, I will never ask you to go with me again." I went with her. At the satsang, I sang with the ladies, read the kirtan enjoyed the snacks and other 'prasad'. As we were walking back home, *Mataji* said," Its six o'clock, your friends must have finished watching the movie", at which I gasped, for I had totally forgotten the movie! This episode I never forgot, for on that day I learnt that the only true companion, parent, nurturer, and saviour is God, and it is to Him that we should always turn when other things fail.

All this stood me in good stead when the time came for the

great transition in my life: from a child to a married woman! Yes we were married on the 21st of January, 1968, in Bombay with great pomp and show. I attended college upto the 16th, on the 17th an '*Akhand Paath*' was organised in the house, the first major ceremony, on the 19th was the '*Shagan*', 20th the '*Baraat*' and 21st was the actual wedding. 21st evening I was in Balbir's house, surrounded by his parents, five elder brothers and sisters-in-law, two elder sisters and their husbands, and several kids. Balbir told me that day that I would have to stop going to college for he was a graduate and could not tolerate that I would be a graduate too."It will hurt my ego if you are as educated as me, a woman ought to be lesser than her husband", he said, and surprisingly the stone on my chest sat quite softly, hurting a lot, but giving me space to swallow too.

Daddy was the only one in the house to say anything to me. He knew how I thought and believed, of my interminable arguments and debates, for I could not accept a dictat, I had to be convinced, everything had to be researched and discussed and only when there was conviction would I follow it. He simply said, "Satvir, in the house where you are going, you are the youngest in the family. Everyone there is older than you. For that alone, you will not argue with or contradict anyone there; even if they are not correct. I have only this to tell you, and I'll never say anything to you after this."

☺☹☹

Chapter 10

Karol Bagh

There I was, in a new place, new family, new parents, new siblings, and new culture. Everything was different. The language was different, the food was different, everyone there was at least twice or thrice my size, and loud to a fault. I could never get a word in, so I was called the quiet one. I was not prepared for anything like this. I had read up thoroughly all about sex in books, and knew that it was necessary when you had to have kids. But I was stunned to learn that it was a major requisite in a marriage. When I asked Mummy why she had not explained it to me, she said that as I was always so knowledgeable, she presumed that I would already know about it. Acceptance came, it had to, and I knew that I had to make a success of this new relationship; I owed it to the family name.

After two weeks, Balbir decided we go on a honeymoon to Ooty. The two days we spent in Bangalore really broke the ice between us, over a shared beer! Balbir asked me if it was okay if he drank beer, he obviously did not know I came from a family of guzzlers, for Daddy was still not into drinking, and Balbir thought we were a family of teetotallers. Actually I thank the Prohibition in Bombay, for otherwise Daddy would have become an alcoholic long back. I told Balbir about the beer with Rory, and it became my very first romantic evening, spent with my husband, sharing frothy Kingfisher beer, and trying to write our names on the thick fizz! I liked Ooty, for it was a lot like my beloved Nainital; the hills are beautiful, and the lake so vast. We enjoyed the lovely riding avenues for I loved horse riding, and we rode for hours, the breeze fragrant with the scent of eucalyptus; and then hours of boating taking turns at the oars. I also began to learn about the birds and bees first hand! On our return after two weeks, Balbir told me that he did not like to live in Bombay as all his friends were in Delhi, and that he had decided to move to Delhi. I had to be a part of that decision. I said okay, if that made him happy, for I knew that whatever else I did, I would just have to keep him happy, I had no other choice. Thankfully, over the years, it actually freely became my choice. So on the 1st of April, 1968, we reached Delhi to settle down here, forever.

From the railway station, we were driven to the house

in Karol Bagh. I had never seen a house like that. It was constructed right up to the road, without any compound or gate, had never been painted, had not a single plant anywhere in or around it. It was designed with a veranda in the middle, with rooms all around which you could count as you walked along, and bathrooms at the end of the rectangle. The kitchen was an unbelievable five by seven, with a chimney! One could build schools and hospitals like that, but a house? Still!

In the early days, my sisters-in -law enthusiastically included me in their conversations, so I got to learn a lot about this new family. My father-in-law was a kind man, very straight-forward, and fair. My mother-in-law could not stop doting on me, but I had a tough time trying to relate to them for they were both older than my grand-parents!

There was so much sex talked about by the sisters-in-law, the eldest two especially. They would mischievously ask each other how they had spent the night, and gloat over their experiences. Their gossip rotated around the lives of their friends and neighbours; who was cheating on the wife or husband and so on. I had never heard about anything called 'porn' before, but I would say what my sisters-in-law talked was 'oral porn'! It appeared to me that people in Karol Bagh did nothing but have sex or talk sex. I had not known then about the terrace culture—how couples feeling the need would escape the eyes of their families and use the ample terrace to make love!

I began escaping their company on some pretext or the other. Luckily I had my books. Soon Gian the wife of Balbir's eldest brother left for London where they lived, and Daler shifted to the ground floor, after a fight with her parents, and she also stopped speaking to me, so I could be my normal self, with mom-in-law for company, the father-in-law being out of bounds for I had to wear 'purdah' from him. Gradually, 'Bhabhiji', Balbir's mother and I became very attached to each other. She became bed-ridden, and I took care of her totally. She became dependant on me, and I too wallowed in the love and blessings I got from her.

Then began the next, the real part of my life. Childhood was over, I realized. On my first trip to Haldwani, I sat with Bauji and told him how in Karol Bagh food was cooked not in the kitchen but in the veranda, that too on a charcoal 'sigri', and I would be expected to cook that way. I was sure he would feel disgusted and do something to save me from that fate, as he had always done. But no! Next morning when I woke up. I found Buaji and Bauji waiting for me with a brand new 'sigri', telling me that Buaji would teach me to light it, clean it and cook on it. I was shocked! MY Bauji could never do this to me. But Bauji said, "Satvir, you must know this, that if I gain in stature or position in society, you may also gain marginally, but you will secure a sound position in society only if B. Asa Singh's (my father-in-law) respect increases, and it is your duty now to get them respected more by everyone, even by us."

With these few words he gave me the direction for my new life.

Karol Bagh was like no place I had ever seen or experienced before. It is a rectangular cluster of houses and lanes, the houses joined together so if you climbed the roof of one house, you could hop across to the next till the end of the road. There is no greenery anywhere except after every six lanes there is a rectangular park, invariably ill-kept. All the houses have a room or two on the terrace, called 'barsati'. As the climate became warmer, everyone began to sleep in the open, as is the custom across North India. There were no lawns or compounds in Karol Bagh, so people had to sleep on the terrace. The barsatis were used to keep the wooden cots in the day, to be taken out in the evening for the family to sleep. As we also started sleeping upstairs, it became apparent that this was a whole new culture. One could look across all the rooftops, and see the activity of all the surrounding families! Some couples would sleep in the barsatis, being shy of the parents; teenagers would be flirting across the terraces, under the garb of making the beds, or hanging out the laundry, or even pretending to study, and lots of teasing and flirting happened too. If you awoke at midnight, the place was a voyeurs' paradise! I think everyone fantasised about making love on the open terrace, on small rickety cots.

But nothing can beat the cool breeze after a sweltering

hot day, coming from the east, called 'Purvayee' or the Easterlies. The fragrant breeze lulled you to sleep. Some nights it would rain, and then we would rush to shift our cots inside the barsati, and the place would be cooler after that. Towards the end of September or early October, I had an amazing experience. I saw what appeared to be some kind of small aircraft flying across the sky, in perfect formation of five or seven or more. It happened on several nights. Across the dark sky this whole formation would fly in striking white, with long wings, in slow but perfect motion. One night I pointed this out to my father-in-law, and he told me this heralded the advent of winter, for these were the Siberian Cranes who flew in every year from Russia and made Delhi their habitat for some months. Wow! Actually, sometimes in the evenings in March or late February, we caught sight of them flying back too. It is so sad that these birds are almost extinct now! The sky those days used to be either pitch dark or bluish-purple in the night, with the stars shining bright, big and small, Venus being the first to show up, and so many clusters like the Great Bear, which the people in Delhi called 'Saptarishi'.

Well, youth is like the sand between the pebbles—it settles down fast. I too settled down and began to be comfortable in Karol Bagh. There was also the convenience of being able to travel to Haldwani and Nainital more often, compared to Bombay. As I started to observe the people in this new place, I realized it would not be easy for me to make friends. Nobody spoke English, and we who did were jeered at. The people by and large were loud and very aggressive in their conversations. I understood that this was because of the almost totally migrant population; few people actually belonged to Delhi. Most of them in Karol Bagh were refugees who had been forced to leave their homes in Pakistan, when the country was partitioned into Pakistan and India. They must have been very resourceful, for soon they all had good businesses running, and managed to become proud house-owners too. But still all their conversations centred around their memories of the golden past; almost all seemed to have been landed aristocrats, and remembered their Muslim friends fondly; it was difficult for them to believe that they could have suffered any harm from them.

The treatment of women was not very different from what it was in the rest of the country, except compared to Bombay, there was too much hypocrisy. There were very few working women, most were housewives not educated beyond the school stage At home they were treated little better than house-maids, but outside they were flaunted like prized possessions, draped in silks and amply bejewelled. Still the women were not only happy, they were actually proud of their husbands and sons! I soon began to observe that these "suppressed, tormented and abused" ladies were in fact behind every major decision taken in their families. They had access to such guile and manipulation that at the end of the day they managed to have their way with the pompous, foolish men thinking that they were ruling the household!

Despite the different culture, and despite the aggressive and hypocritical nature of the people, I discovered a certain warmth in them; for instance, they'd be quick to invite even strangers into their homes, and a casual visit would turn into a lunch date ("How can you go without eating?") Unfamiliar women were addressed as "Bhabhi" unlike "Bhenji", used in Bombay. Once, someone I had been introduced to told me that he would love to come to my house and share my husband's 'parathas', which was explained to me to mean that he was admiring me! Such a merry-go-round, couldn't he say it straight? But this was Delhi.

The Delhiites love for 'Tandoori' food is well known. Tandoori chicken, fish, and cottage cheese—the possibilities are endless. What I loved most was the corner 'tandoor wala', to whom we would take the kneaded dough, and he would create crisp tandoori rotis for us in his clay oven for just a few paisa each ! These rotis were such a delight, they would turn a simple meal of 'Daal' or vegetables into a king's spread. The ladies loved them as they were spared the ordeal of making them. They added a sparkle to dull winter evenings when we ladies huddled in front of the T.V. Long summer afternoons became a picnic with tandoori 'Aloo parathas' or 'missi rotis' served with butter, chutney, curds and jugs of 'lassi'. These men also took away the tedium of rolling out chapattis day after day!

Many winter afternoons, as well as summer evenings were spent on the green lawns of India Gate. Driving around Delhi was difficult because of bad traffic, but some areas were a treat because of the greenery. The beautifully maintained lawns at the 'Buddha Jayanti Gardens' were a delight; one could walk for hours there for they were never crowded. One summer day there was a sudden downpour and Balbir and I celebrated by dancing on those lawns while digging into juicy mangoes, Indian style, holding the mango in our hand and sucking out the juicy pulp!

Security was not a hazard back then, and often we would see dignitaries, politicians, and other famous people enjoying the various parks. I realized Delhiites were basically lovers of outdoor places.

What would I not give now, to experience those wonderful nights on the rooftops, gazing at the starry sky, hundreds of poetry lines crossing the mind, hundreds getting created new, awaiting the sight of the Great Siberian Cranes!

Looking back now, after forty odd years, I can see the stirrings of a new awakening in me, maybe childhood was saying goodbye and youth was making its impish appearance; the carefully nurtured bud at last getting ready to open and flower, move into the next, ripe, mature part of such a long life! The most productive part of my life (pun intended) was beginning.

A new schooling, a new education was now needed. I realized I needed to learn about sex, to begin with, and ordered a book brought out by the Readers' Digest titled, "Every Thing You Always Wanted To Know About Sex". Balbir was shocked to see that a book could cost seventy rupees. Then I bought books on reproduction, but they were medical textbooks, giving me great knowledge, but of no use to me as a wife. The Readers' Digest book was more informative, but quite clinical. Sometime later I read 'Surrogate Wife' by Masters & Johnson, and learnt for the first time that sex contained so much passion! Up till then I believed it to be merely a physical duty.

Six months after the marriage, the terrible question began to be asked every month, "Have you had your periods again?" I was terrified. I was almost declared barren when a year passed and I had still not conceived. People commented that it was so sad, for I was a nice person otherwise. My mother-in-law started to send me to quacks, who were filthy and unhygienic to say the least. I was so disgusted. I soon found a good gynaecologist and convinced my mother-in-law that the doctor was the person to help me, not a quack. I showed her the medical books, and even explained to her the possible causes and their treatments. After that I was nothing less than a qualified medical doctor to her. She would tell everyone that I was actually a doctor, who could not complete her studies, and would never believe me when

I told her that was not so. She became inseparable from me. I felt proud that she trusted only me, though this gave rise to much jealousy among my other sisters-in-law!

Around this time my mom's family created a major scandal in Bombay. My cousin Kulbir, an engineering student at the V J T I, was discovered to be in love with a Catholic girl. His family was very upset, but he was so adamant that they shifted him to live and work in Jammu with his uncles, just to separate him from Nirupa, his girl friend, nipping his brilliant career so cruelly! I was aghast, and both Balbir and I called him up in Jammu to say that we supported him, but he was helpless, penniless, and had been barred from talking on the phone also. The manipulative, dictatorial elders, probably did not know that 'absence makes the heart grow fonder'. I would often take messages from Nirupa and call Kulbir in Jammu and convey whatever was possible in the three minutes of the trunk call. He was shattered, but not down, and decided to struggle. After some months, Kulbir escaped from Jammu to return to Bombay, and when his parents denied him entry to their house, slept at railway platforms, lived off friends, earned scholarships from the college, did whatever needed to continue his engineering studies. During this period, Daddy once met him somewhere and got him home to live at our place, but Mummy revolted very passionately, and going with her family, asked him to leave. I was shocked at her decision, for I really loved Kulbir and respected his decision to stand by his love. Anyway, once he had the engineering degree, nothing could stop him. He landed a good job, married Nirupa, and now lives in New York, with his three charming daughters.

Chapter 11

The Nursing Station

Two years after my marriage, my mother-in-law needed an operation to remove cataract from her eyes, and we believed that the best doctors were in Bombay. So we went to Bombay, where I stayed with her for three months. The operation was successful and her recovery was perfect. But I had an amazing experience while I stayed at the nursing home with her. The experience made me mature, and sensitive to the tribulations of city life.

In almost all nursing homes, the pattern is the same; the peaceful, sleepy dawn gives way to a burst of activity after six o'clock in the morning. First the cooks start to clang the trays and cups and saucers, to get the tea ready; then the bearers rush into the rooms of all the patients, opening the door with great force, pulling aside the curtains with a 'whoosh', putting down the tea tray while saying 'Good Morning' with gusto, to make sure the patients and attendants come wide awake! Gradually the other staff begin their rounds. The nurse takes the temperature, blood-pressure, and checks the respiration all together, then rushes to complete the patients' sponging, brushing, combing, and changing of the bed linen, for she has to complete her work before the Day-Nurses come. It may be uncomfortable for the patients, but it has to be done, and the patients are like babies handled in a matter-of-fact way.

Sister Joyce steps out of the lift at 8 o'clock sharp, as she has been doing everyday for the last twelve years, fresh and crisp in her white sari wishing everyone 'Good Morning', starting with the liftman, the sweeper, for after the nurses have done their course of morning care, the sweepers are at work cleaning, sweeping, and vigorously mopping with their specially scented liquids. She is bright and cheerful, and has a very comforting smile; she seems to be quite content with her life too. "It's easy in this place, there are only eye surgeries happening here, which are not too uncomfortable or painful. The tough ones are elsewhere; trauma patients, terminal patients, cancer wards, my God! Everyone here knows they will be fine soon. You cheer up too, come on. Join us later for lunch". Bhabhiji was staying in the hospital not because she needed but so that she did not feel less important with a quick discharge.

There was a special nurse for her all the time, so my presence was only decorative really, and I had lots of time to chat with the staff and other patients and their relatives; Roshan, our special day-nurse, would pamper my mother-in-law, feeding her lovingly, listening to all her anecdotes, or pretending to, freshening her up in the evenings to look bright for the visitors. But she was firm when the Doctor's orders had to be followed, then 'Maaji', as my mother-in-law was addressed by them, could grumble away but Roshan would not give in. I admired the way she managed a difficult old lady, but I was not really comfortable with her when we met outside at the Nursing Station, where we stopped for a chat now and then. Some days she was very friendly, some days she was sarcastic, and sometimes she appeared very depressed. However, when she entered her patient's room it was as if a mask came on. I was puzzled and wondered what was bothering her!

Ruby was the most caring nurse in the whole place. Actually, it being a small nursing-home specialising in eye surgeries, nurses were the people you met during the day; the doctors were seen briefly in the morning, giving instructions or ordering a discharge, and some minutes in the night, if at all. Ruby looked after all the patients' records and complaints, and did the nursing for those patients who were alone. It was actually a lot to do, for I saw her running from feeding one patient to helping another to relieve himself, helping someone to sit up, or reading the papers for another. Maria another nurse did the routine jobs like taking temperature, giving medicines and, writing down the records of each patient.

Bhabhiji one day dozed off after her breakfast, and I made my way to the Nursing Station. I would sometimes take snacks along to share and hoped to get some Parsi buns or '*Vada Pao*' from them. Once I complimented Ruby, "I wonder how this place would function without you. I heard Mr Seth telling his wife that you are the one actually responsible for his recovery, even more than Dr Amir. He wished he had a daughter like you, and also that if he was wealthy he would leave everything to you. He was praising you so much." "Oh that's nice," said Ruby "People do say nice things to get the best from us. Once they leave, they forget our name. Most don't even recognise me without my nurses' uniform! But I don't mind; I do my duty well and that's it."

I said, "but tell me, what is the problem with Roshan. She's so moody; sometimes she is so cheerful that our room brightens up when she walks in but sometimes she is so unfriendly. I really want to know. Obviously she has some problem in her life and I want to be able to help her. She is so young. Is she married?"

"You bet! She's almost always been married. When they were kids, she and Dara, it was decided that they would be married when they grew up. They are cousins you know, and among Parsis it's frequently done. They have been each others' best friends, and been in love since childhood. Their wedding was the high point of their lives. Actually, Dara is my cousin too. But it's so sad to see them now!"

"What's happened now?"

"I should not be talking about this. Roshan does not like it. So please don't tell anyone. Roshan hasn't been able to have a baby, and it's very important to Dara that they have a child."

"But she's so young; she'll have a child bye and bye. Some women have them late sometimes".

"She's been trying for so long. She does special duties to make money for her treatment with Dr. Soonawala. He's the best but most expensive."

"He is the best doctor in Bombay certainly. That man is said to have worked miracles with many childless couples."

"He has tried hard with Roshan. See how fat she has become with all his hormone treatments. But it's been no use. She feels quite hopeless now. And Dara has started to talk of leaving her if she does not have a child."

"That's awful! How can he think of leaving his childhood love for something that is not her fault? They can adopt a child, if they are so desperate."

"No they can't. Any one out of the Parsi bloodline will not be allowed to receive the inheritance due to Dara. Dara's uncle owns three flats in 'Bomanji Wadi', and since this uncle has no children, he will bequeath these to Dara and his sisters. If Dara has no child, all the flats will go to his sisters. This is the real reason for Dara's desperation. Also by now he's become obsessed with having a child—he thinks of nothing else."

"Unbelievable! Just to be able to inherit a flat, he is ready to leave his wife? What if his second wife also does not have kids?"

"My dear, in Bombay, for middle-class people, a flat is more important than partners or lovers! It is very sad"

I came away feeling as if I was directly impacted by Roshan's experience. Actually I was, with everyone among my in-laws being sarcastic about my not having conceived yet! I decided to be very kind to her. Back in the room, I fussed over Bhabhiji, while thinking how shallow our most intimate and dependable relationships really are!

Next day I didn't leave the room, the previous day's outing having been so disturbing. I blamed myself for being so curious about peoples' lives. After Bhabhiji had had her evening tea, I sent Roshan to have hers, and when she returned, I carried sandwiches and 'mawa cakes' to the nursing-station to share with the nurses. Ruby was not there, so Joyce and Maria had tea with me. I felt quite talkative, having been quiet since morning. The other two smiled politely, but I could see Joyce getting restless. I teased her,

"You're missing your dear patients and are in such a hurry to be with them? Another two days and God knows when we'll meet again. The experience in this nursing-home has been so good because of you kind nurses."

They said, "We too are glad to have met you. Rarely are patients or their family members so friendly with us. You are so kind. You take out time to talk to us and share food with us." Joyce quietly left for her duties. I told Maria, "Joyce could have sat awhile; I am also going to the room soon."

I looked into the room and saw that Bhabhiji had dozed off again. I walked up and down the corridor, looking at the visitors coming to visit their relatives or friends. Nobody came to see Bhabhiji that day, so I was quite bored. Our family members came only after eight, on their way back from office. Joyce was rushing through her work—she was an entirely different person from the one I saw in the morning. She was impatient with the staff, almost irritable, and obviously in a great hurry. I met Ruby in the corridor, and asked her, "what's happened to Joyce all of a sudden? Where's the calm, composed and cheerful lady who walks in like a fresh breeze?"

"This is the evening Joyce for you!" She said. "The lady is in a tearing hurry. This is the only time of the day she gets to meet her husband and that too for just a few minutes. So naturally she is in a hurry".

"What do you mean, this is the only time she meets her husband? Don't they live together?"

"They do live together, of course but they are both working different shifts; she does day-shift and he does night-shift. She catches the local train from Grant Road, and gets down at Dadar, and her husband comes from Andheri, where they live, and also gets down at Dadar, where they spend some minutes together, before he takes the Harbour Line to Parel where he works in a mill, and she takes the train to Andheri to go home. John cooks the dinner before leaving and Joyce cooks the lunch in the morning. It works well for them. Sundays they are both free and they make up for the whole week—they eat together, go to church, buy groceries, cook together and relax."

"And what about their children?"

"They have no kids. Before they married, when they were seeing each other, Joyce had some problem and had to have her uterus removed. So they cannot have kids."

"And John still married her?"

"Yes. Their love is something wonderful. John says, so long as they have each other, nothing else matters. You should see them on weekends; they are like a newly-wed couple! God bless them."

"They may not have all the luxuries, but they have love, precious love!"

I heard Roshan calling me, so I went to our room to see what could be the matter. Bhabhiji was fretting that no one had come to see her, so to pacify her I said that there was a big rally at Shivaji Park, so maybe because of the traffic the other people from home could not come. Anyway, Papaji and Balbir would come in a while.

After Bhabhiji had had her dinner, I was again free, and loitered towards the nursing station. Only Ruby was there, changing to go home. After getting into her dress, she began to make-up her face, and I looked on surprised, as she dexterously blended the foundation on her face. I felt she was really particular about her looks when she was to meet her husband. Then she put on skin coloured leggings, complete with panty-hose, while talking to me. Then she put on a pair of false eye-lashes, and her eyes looked beautiful. I looked on astonished as she pasted on a set of false painted long nails. I could not stop myself asking her what this was all about?

She said, "Don't be shocked, I'll tell you the truth. Three nights a week I dance the Cabaret at the Hotel Nataraj, the only place in Bombay to have a Cabaret show."

"I can't believe it! You're a nurse, in such a noble profession, and from such a good family. How could you fall into this terrible trap? It's so disgraceful doing a performance like that in a hotel."

"Well my brother wanted to become a doctor. My father could not afford it, and since I am a good dancer, when someone mentioned this opening, I thought I might try it. I spoke to the priest at our temple and he told me that, any work done for a good cause is God's work, only I must do it like work and maintain the goodness of my own character. My parents objected, but where else could we hope to get so much money? So I convinced them. My brother's happiness when he becomes a doctor and fulfils his ambition will make up for everything. I have to get going; the car must have come from the Hotel." Then she winked at me and said, "Come there sometime to see what 'luxury' means, and how people throw money to see some skin!"

"See you tomorrow," I said, my mind not quite digesting what I had seen.

The next day we got our discharge and returned to Delhi.

Two years later, I was back in the same Nursing-Home, as Bhabhiji needed the surgery for her other eye. Once again, I walked around to the Nursing-Station. No one from the previous staff was there. After a while Ruby came and recognised me and we started chatting

Over tea and biscuits, I asked her, "Do you meet Roshan. How is she getting along?"

Ruby let out a sigh and said, "Well you remember her and her problem? Dara left her and married a young widow that his mother found for him."

"So sad! Poor thing, and where is she working now?"

"She's not working anywhere; she does not need to work anymore. Actually she married Dara's uncle, you know, the one with the three flats. His sympathy for her turned to love, and he decided to sacrifice his bachelorhood. She is quite happy now, for no one can love as intensely as an old bachelor who suddenly finds love so late in his life! I'm really happy for her."

"And how is Joyce? Is her husband still doing night-duty?"

"The mill where he worked in shut down like many others, and he never found another job. Now Joyce works in a Hospital near her home in the day, and does special nurse's duty in the night to make ends meet. She gets to meet John for a couple of hours sometimes if she gets leave. John's almost lost his mind being out of work, and is very lonely. He is irritable, depressed and cross all the time. Poor Joyce!"

My eyes clouded over, and I felt very sad. The twists and turns of life! Only God knows what is in store for us.

I looked at Ruby for a long time. I hesitated, but then cautiously asked her how her life was doing. "Oh! My life is just the same; nurse by day, Cabaret-dancer by night; my brother finished his MBBS, and married his girl friend, joining her father's practice. So now I don't dance for my brother's studies, but I work for my parents' medicines and treatments and other needs, my brother having moved away from us. That's the only change in my life."

"Did you not think of marriage yourself, I mean its time you settled down too."

She got up to leave to attend to her patients saying, "Grow up darling! Who will want to marry a Cabaret dancer, a part of the scum of society? Tell me?"

Sadly, Bhabhiji could not have that second surgery for she suffered a heart attack a day before it was scheduled. She succumbed to it a week later, leaving me lonely and sad.

Chapter 12

A Different Father

After three years of my marriage, my mother-in-law died, after giving me so much love. She would say, "Satbir, I bless you with all my heart. Why does God not answer my prayers? You will surely be blessed with many children, only I will not be around to see them." After her death my life felt empty, for we had been constant companions. I became depressed. Then my father-in-law offered to take me to office with him. He said, "My eyesight is getting weaker. If you join me in the office, you can help me, and also you will not feel lonely." I loved that, for even as a child I was used to go to the petrol pump and to our Motor spare parts shop with *Bauji* and Daddy. Papaji had earned his millions by trading in old motor spare parts. He had been comfortable in Peshawar to which he belonged, but when the World War II ended, the receding armies left behind a gold mine in the shape of army trucks, jeeps, tanks and other transport, mostly in heaps of junk in the far eastern state of Assam. Enterprising businessmen like Papaji and even *Bauji* rushed there to buy up all they could for they could sell these at high profits. Papaji used to tell me that stuff like bearings which they bought for a rupee, would be air-lifted from Calcutta to Delhi, and be sold for twenty rupees! There is this interesting episode about both Papaji from Peshawar and *Bauji* from Haldwani having gone to Dimapur in Assam, living as guests of a common relative, Mr. Gurmukh Singh. There were a lot of tyres for sale, and both were desperate to buy them, leading to an unpleasant situation for the local host, for he could not decide which of the two to help. Then one evening over drinks, they realized that Papaji needed only the metal rims inside the tyres and *Bauji* needed only the rubber tyres to export to Iran, where *Mataji'* brother had a flourishing business. So they both shared the lot, and even paid half the price! After my marriage they would both remember the incident fondly, and cheer each other.

Soon after Papaji had built his fortune, all his sons joined in the business and within ten years they had business outlets in Calcutta, Delhi, Bombay and London, for the same post war scenario prevailed in Europe. Balbir's eldest brother made his base in London, from where he would ship to

Bombay the goods procured from all over Europe. They had also built houses in all these cities, and owned many other prime properties too.

When I began working with Papaji, he was buying old trucks from army auctions, getting them dismantled part by part, down to each nut and bolt, and selling each part in different markets. He was a very straight businessman, a man of principles. He always insisted that labourers ought to be paid their due before their sweat had dried. He also taught me that for a businessman it was important that his assets be evenly distributed—one fourth of the assets should be stock, one fourth cash in hand, one fourth property, and a fourth in gold investments. It made perfect sense for there were very few saving schemes available apart from Fixed Deposits in banks. After he had made a successful bid at the auctions and paid for the goods, I would handle the job of getting the trucks transported to our place, getting the labour for dismantling them, and then arranging wagons with the railways for sending the bulky parts like the driver's cabin and the chassis, to Bombay, from where they were exported to Iran and Singapore.

One day, though, Papaji took me totally by surprise; he had invited a friend and his wife to live in our house for some days. Actually the friend was a widower and had recently remarried a widow in a match arranged by some social workers. He was quite affluent and owned many flats in

Bombay, but his sons objected to the remarriage and insulted his new wife, so he took her and left home, and Papaji offered to put him up for some days till he could find new accommodation. Now Papaji asked me if I would have any objection if he decided to remarry. I said no, but wondered because I remembered how much he had loved Bhabhiji and how many months he had wept when she expired. He must have guessed my thoughts for he said, "I can never love anyone as much as I loved your mother-in-law, and no one can take her place, but I do need companionship, and one's sexual needs are real, and they should be met rightly within the sanctity of marriage." He was so honest, straight and simple! As I had noticed the happiness his friend shared with his new wife, I realized Papaji could be happy too, so I told him, "Please feel free to do what you like. Balbir and I will respect your decision and be happy for you." He was happy, but sadly it was not to be, for Balbir's brother in Bombay, objected and though Papaji did not much care for his opinion, he allowed himself to get manipulated into investing his money in properties in London where my eldest brother-in-law lived. Three years later Papaji left for London, never to return, for there he had a heart attack that proved fatal.

While I was enjoying working with Papaji the impatient wait for a baby was a constant tension. None of the gynaecologists I went to really helped me. It was on a trip to Hyderabad visiting my mother's brother, 'Moni Uncle, that he took us for a pilgrimage to the Gurudwara 'Nanak Jheera' in the town of Bidar in Karnataka. My uncle told Balbir he believed that whatever we asked of God in this place was granted, so we prayed for a child to be born to us. Fortunately, the very month we returned I conceived, and when the tests reported positive, my heart missed a beat, and I felt closer to God than ever! My heart was full of wonder; something I had believed to be impossible had come true and I would ultimately get to be a mother! Of course God is everywhere but since then a special attachment got created for 'Nanak Jheera Sahib', and that is where we go to pray for everything, where we know we will never be disappointed, Balbir's faith in that place is unshakable.

I could not share my joy with anyone immediately. I had to wait till next morning to book a trunk call to Mummy in Bombay, for up to eight o'clock in the morning we paid only half the charges of a call, and got connected sooner too. My mother-in-law had expired. Daler aunty never spoke to me after the fight she had with my in-laws. Her son Ruby remained my only friend in the family. He defied his mother but never let up in his friendship with me, and we love and respect each other even today. I waited for Ruby to return from school as I was dying to share my good news with someone, and Ruby was genuinely happy.

The baby's expected date of arrival was beginning June.

By the end of April all of Balbir's nephews and nieces had come down from Bombay, for every year they would spend two months of their vacations with us. On the third of May, I had pain in my abdomen, but I never thought it could be labour pains, as the date was still far off. I simply took a pain killer. I had been smarting from a relative having remarked that we Bombay girls could only show off by speaking English, we could never learn to make '*Tandoori rotis*'. So despite my pain, I went off to buy a new *Tandoor*, and catching hold of a cousin, spent the afternoon learning to bake rotis on it. That night we had homemade *tandoori rotis*, and then I played cards with the children, as my own younger sisters were there too. Around four in the morning, I woke up screaming with pain. Balbir asked me what had happened, and I said, "I don't know". Bewildered, we called Ruby and he drove us to the hospital. When we reached there the staff rushed me to the labour room. The doctor was so annoyed. She told me if I had not reached there right then, I may have delivered on the way. Forty five minutes later Chingi was born, God's greatest blessing to me. But I'll never forget the loneliness I felt as I had had no one to advise me that I was having labour pains! We were not prepared at all for the delivery and we had no clothes for the baby. Papaji cried with happiness as he missed my mother-in-law and how happy she would have been. He took out the fabric in which the Guru Granth Sahibji was wrapped and sent it to the hospital to wrap the newborn. Later Balbir's elder sister came and helped me through the next week and Mummy also came from Bombay carrying loads of gifts for Chingi.

After fifteen months my second son Ricky was born, doubling our happiness. Papaji kept saying, "These are all your Bhabhiji's blessings." Some months later he left for London, where he breathed his last. In October nineteen seventy eight, Chintu, my third son was born. He was really pampered by the elder two! Amazingly, before I knew it, I was pregnant again, and eleven months later Babboo, the youngest was born.

The next fifteen years passed like a dream, and when I awoke, Chingi had cleared the entrance to join the Delhi College of Engineering and Babboo was in class six; four lively, intelligent, headstrong, fun-loving and independent young men! We were all so happy.

Chapter 13

'I Love You'

I have on the whole enjoyed my life with Balbir; the negatives are very few, though the human mind loves to dwell on them. Balbir begins each day by thanking God. We have never compromised when we wanted to have fun. We have enjoyed picnics, travelling, the hills and the beaches, the movies and snacks, the *chai* and *bhajias* as well as the fish and whiskey! We had an understanding that if one of us enjoyed something and the other did not, then we would go ahead alone or with friends and enjoy it. We both gave each other ample space and freedom. Life has been a long romance, and continues to be so, thank God!

Balbir is a simple person; long conversations, logical explanations, arguments, convincing others are not his style. He simply makes his statement, and that's it. He has a heart of gold, is very loving, honest and humble, but very demanding once he decides what he wants. You just have to do it. But love makes you accept many things, and for the man you love, you compromise on many things. Sometimes I feel I have been cheating him so much, for I have often worked around him cleverly so as not to hurt his ego, but achieving for the kids what I felt would be better for them. I was ambitious for my kids to get a good education, an all round education. I wanted them to think like free individuals, make their own decisions, and be responsible for those decisions. I wanted them to choose their beliefs, find their convictions, choose the life they wanted to lead and be what they wanted to be.

Many times I failed. I was often not strong enough and my kids suffered too. There was conflict between their ambitions, the freedom I had taught them to live with and Balbir's ambition that all his sons should grow up and join him in his business. The elder two aligned their ambitions with his but Sarabjit's interests were different. The family was not ready for a struggling son with an indefinite future even though he was very confident. I could not take the stand for him. There were financial constraints too, that we all learned to live with, and learnt to rise above, and be cheerful in spite of. Today all the boys are doing well in their chosen careers, and I am a happy and proud mother.

One grows spiritually too, and social pressures are not

so daunting for me anymore. When Sarabjit decided upon an unconventional marriage, I was able to make up my mind quite independently. Though shaken at first, I asked myself, 'did a girl not have the right to marry someone she loved, even if he was of a different religion? If she happened to be older did she not have the right to find happiness?' And I decided to support their relationship, even when it came to being a live-in one. I was sure I could stand up for them, in spite of social pressures. When confronted with a dominating and incompatible wife, Sandeep was confused but I was still able to make my own decision and broke off with her before anyone else could.

Was I becoming wiser? Unfortunately, by the time we become wise it's time to go away! In life one never really gets to settle scores; we go away from this world taking some, leaving some; up with some, down with others; never quits

Chapter 14

Daddy Speaks!

The round-the-clock rum does not even make an effort to cloud my brain. There's no fog, nothing is clouded ever, there's only a mild warmth around my memories. Why isn't Satvir here yet? She said she'll come on Monday. But maybe she said next Monday; I'll make a call and find out; her number is on the paper here. Let me get an egg to eat; I need to eat something warm.

You were there Satvir, sitting with *Bauji*, when I came home suddenly from Bombay as I was homesick; it was May, and you and your Mummy were gone for more than a month. You saw me leave my bag outside *Bauji's* room and come in happily, happy to meet you all again. *Bauji* looked me up and down, his eyes piercing through me, saying what he left unsaid. "Are you home early for lunch, Trilochan," he said, pretending to mistake me for my twin brother. He actually meant to say, "So! You've left the business unattended in Bombay and come away travelling two nights, just to be with your wife; you're soooo weak and emotional!" I bent my head down and said, "I am Trilok, *Bauji*. I've come from Bombay because there were strikes and the shop was closed." I bowed to touch his feet, but went inside the house without waiting for a blessing. I had recently lost your younger sister to an incurable disease called Meningitis, and I just could not bear to live without you and your mother. Still, I forgot *Bauji's* sarcasm when I met everybody.

That year, the first children's magazine had been published in India, '*Parag*', and I had got you an issue from Bombay. You were very happy as it was a Hindi magazine, and as yet your English was not so good. The next few days I took you for long walks, to Kathgodam, Ranibag, or across the 'Gola' bridge in the shady woods, answering all your silly and intelligent questions, both of us so happy. Then we all went back to Bombay together.

Bombay I have always loved but Allahabad is still my first love. I should never have left Allahabad. Reading the poets—Keats, Tennyson, Shelly; the Historians—Marx, Lenin and the Russian writers, discussing them over endless glasses of tea, Comrades all around, soaked in communist Philosophy— that was the life! All Communist heroes were our heroes. Our teachers were icons of society, famous and dedicated people like Harivansh Rai Bachchan, and Sri Shankar Dayal Sharma, who later became the President of India. Dr Radhakrishnan was from Aligarh University, but often came over as a guest lecturer, and the classes would overflow with students.

Even then *Bauji's* sudden visit to the college shook my confidence. His personality did that to me. All my pride in my academic achievements simply turned to nothing in his presence! It seemed he was not interested in my studies, and instead asked me to get ready and go with him to the '*bazaar*'. I was surprised as he took me to some big shops, and ordered new clothes for me; not the ones I regularly wore, but very fine trousers and shirts, and also suits to be stitched in the latest fashion. I did not even dare to ask him the occasion for all this! Before leaving, he told me that my marriage had been fixed and all this shopping was towards the preparation for it. I barely managed the courage to ask who the girl was. I was told that she was the daughter of S Jagat Singh of Dehradun, and that she was both pretty and educated.

I was torn between uncertainity, fears and joy. All my encounters with women, except my cousins and aunts, had happened only in literature or fantasy. I felt helpless thinking how I would face my bride!

The marriage took place in Dehradun, with several parties thrown for us, the best being the one hosted by

'Rai Sahib Kirpa Ram' who owned the 'Savoy Hotel' in Mussourie. He told me that he had been a modest school teacher in Pakistan, and my father-in-law had taken him to Iran, taught him to trade and made him a very rich man, for which he was deeply grateful to him. I was gratified; it seemed a good match for *Bauji's* status. We soon returned to Haldwani with Daler. She was all that I could have imagined an ideal woman to be! She was sensitive, caring, friendly, loving, obedient, religious, respectful, and unselfish. She slowly took on the responsibility of the whole family, even our extended family of *Buaji, Taaiji*, and my cousins. Trilochan grew very fond of her and she too loved him like a sister. I still had to complete my law course, so I went back to the University to finish my L.L.B. Within a year our first child, Satvir, was born. She was the greatest wonder of my life. I never tired of carrying her around in my arms—her very existence gave me so much happiness and peace.

Bauji had already decided to start a business in Bombay, and in 1950, the year Satvir was born, had bought a shop in Girgaum Road, Bombay, near the Portuguese Church, to trade in motor spare parts. Several Sikh gentlemen were doing the same. Bombay was identified as a potentially booming business centre. I continued in Haldwani for a couple of years after my Law degree. I loved walking to Kathgodam to the Petrol Pump, loved the slow pace of work, ample time to read and write, for I had started writing too, and as important people were in touch with my family, I enjoyed the company of intelligent people. Daler was there, my two aunts were there, and soon in 1953, I had my second daughter, 'Bamboo'.

My responsibilities increased and I had to go to Bombay to work as there were bigger profits to be made there.

Life changed suddenly. The spring in my step gave way to heavy feet, gradually. My shoulders started drooping with the responsibility of two 'daughters'. I was thrown out of my cocoon, my Kathgodam, my Haldwani, where everything was 'ours', the hills, the hill-people, the hill towns, the lorries and buses, the labourers and coolies, the Railway Station, the Banks, all were 'ours', and we belonged to them. I never needed to have money in my pocket as it never mattered. If I walked through the town I was respected and people greeted me affectionately.

In Bombay I missed all that. I stayed in hostels and in small one-room accommodations, and my focus was on making money. Being an active member of the Communist Party, I soon made the acquaintance of many learned and politically active people. Also the people in the 'Motor-market' were friendly, almost all being of the same '*Biradari*' sharing roots in Punjab.

Since childhood I had been a confident person; I knew what I had to do and I would do it well, whether it was study, or work. I still had that confidence—I knew we would make a lot of money. Trilochan and I were working together, and our team-work was perfect.

I only become nervous when I thought of *Bauji*; his scorn, his look of censure never left me. I was always going to be answerable to him, no matter how well I did; his frown would still be there, and his caustic comments too.

We worked hard and money began to pour in! We were very fortunate to have such great education. Not just the degrees but basic education of life. We had had the opportunity of seeing '*Tayaji*' running a huge business, building railway stations, roadways, bridges, transporting, contracting, and *Bauji* following in his footsteps. Our education gave us an edge over others. We were able to discover new countries manufacturing better cheaper and newer products, whose demand would increase in India and we were able to send back money to *Bauji*, and he was very happy and proud—after all it was his decision to start the business in Bombay. We soon became a name to reckon with in the Motor-market. I heard people telling their growing sons, "Go and sit awhile at Trilok's shop; you'll learn something."

What more could I ask for from God? A caring and popular wife, lovely children, three huge houses in Khar, and soon God even blessed me with a son!

Life went on as it does. Wise men go on living with their own special efforts and contributions to society, using wisely their time on earth. They live in total harmony with nature, creating a benign and peaceful society. I lived a very ordinary life. I got my share of laughs and woes, success and triumph, struggles and tragedies. I lost my father, whom I loved and admired, my wife, and a young daughter. These were all terrible blows.

Satvir has come. It is evening and I am looking forward to going with her for a drive. I wait for Satvir to have tea and tell her, "can we go for a drive till Ranibagh? This boy Shankar who stays with me is bored, so I promised to take him." We go driving up my favourite hills, and I breathe the scented air again. We decide to stop, as it will get dark soon. I cannot eat anything, so I have some tea, and Shankar gets *Bhajias* to eat, and we drive back. I am tired, but happy. I'll sleep and tomorrow I'll ask Satvir to take me up earlier so that I can walk a little on the slopes.

So we keep driving up the slopes every day, sometimes twice! I am very happy Satvir has come. She is driving the car, and I am satisfied with the short outings as the hills never fail to thrill me. But I am too weak, too frail to walk, even with Shankar's help, so he helps me to settle back in the car. I am grateful to them both for making my day so pleasant. I want to bless them. I try to raise my hand to pat the top of Satvir head in blessing, but cannot raise it high enough. My eyes swell with tears, I don't know if Satvir understands; it doesn't matter!

Five days now, we have been doing the same trips and I am feeling very happy. After some days I get the feeling that it's time for Satvir to go back. Nobody says it, but I come to know. We chat a lot in the afternoons every day. Today I call Satvir and confide in her, "Satvir, I am being totally honest with you now, I just do not want to live anymore!" I can see she is shocked, but as she looks into my eyes, she understands, and fights the urge to say anything; she knows she cannot offer false sympathy or concern, we are not like that. "I absolutely do not want to live anymore. I just want to die. I am ninety years old and I have lived enough." Satvir says, "you are only eighty, and" but I cut her short. "What difference does it make whether it is ninety or eighty? I actually stopped living the day your mother went away twenty five years ago. When I went to put her ashes in the Godavari River, I kept on walking into the water, with the urn in my arms, till I was up to my chin in the water; I never wanted to come back. I was gone with Daler. Then I looked back and saw Gullu standing behind, and I returned; I had duties towards my son that I had to fulfil. I've done my best, and I have loved you all. But I do not want to live anymore."

Satvir bent her head down accepting my feelings. Next day she left. I was lying in bed and did not raise my head when she came to say goodbye. We simply looked into each others' eyes and with a wave of my hand, I sent her away. Forever!

We're standing in the twilight,
It's going to get dark
Come meet me for a while,
Let me look into your face;
Your honest eyes, straight brow,
Deep feelings, belonging, old pangs,
Now betrayed.
You'll remember too,
My eyes, searching for you in yours,
In the last fragments of sunlight
Before we are lost to the dark.
When we stand in the twilight,
The only way to go.
Is to walk into the dark!

* * * * *

Nearly a month after this, Daddy suffered a stroke. He was alone at home with the servant, and called Gullu's name before he collapsed. He got medical aid promptly, but slipped into coma. They discovered that he had been suffering from hydrocephalus for a long time, thus explaining his eccentricities, and obstinacy, and irritability. The last years of his life had been torture. His erratic behaviour and bad temper were attributed to his alcoholism, which he suffered from too. It began with a swig of *Bauji's* scotch poured into his evening tea when he was in school, just as mine did with a spoonful of brandy in milk; both our poisons were the same!

But his memory was sharp as ever, so no one imagined he could be having a neurotic disorder.

But now it was terrible to see him thus, being fed, washed, dressed, and taken out in the sun, all without his permission. We would sit by him for hours, watching, praying, helpless too. I could have cried buckets, my heart was so full, but in Daddy's presence, it was not done! I packed all his books in cartons and I hugged every carton, the way I would have hugged my parents, only, with them, 'it was not done'. I made short trips to Delhi as I had responsibilities at home. On the 10th of February 2010, when I was driving back to Haldwani, and for the first time in four months Gullu had left his side to go to Agra for some work that Daddy had his final seizure, I'm not sure if I'm saying the right thing, but I think he finally had to be with Mummy. I reached Daddy's side at seven in the evening and wished him. The next moment he was still—absolutely still.

Chapter 15

Never An Ending

When I was growing up in Haldwani, I believed that this town would always remain as big or as small as it was; actually it was a logical belief as there was no way it could go beyond its boundaries. Upwards, one could only go into the hills after the Kathgodam station towards the north; behind the railway tracks on the east was the 'Gaula' river, followed by the woods, like a natural boundary; downstream towards the south there were fields and woods leading to 'Lalkuan' the next town, on the road to Bareilly. Between Lalkuan and Rudrapur on the west, the Great University of Pantnagar had been built, joined by the Rampur Road, ending Haldwani's limits on that side; and any way Rampur Road led through the region called 'Tanda', which was thickly wooded and filled with gangs of active dacoits too. The road was patrolled by the army, and all traffic on the road was stopped strictly at five o'clock in the evening, for fear of the '*Dakus*'! To the west were the thick jungles towards the town of '*Kala Dhungi*', famous for Jim Corbett's house, and till the River Kosi near Ramnagar, and on towards the hills. These woods were full of wild animals, and one often heard of villagers being attacked by a tiger, or a child carried away by a hyena!

How wrong I was! After Nainital lost its greenery to multi-coloured construction, Haldwani too expanded unbelievably. The authorities in this small town crossed the river Gaula and cleared the forest for cultivation. Hundreds of acres were cleared to create fields for an "Open Jail"—an experimental project where prisoners were to be kept free within the boundaries of the lush green fields, leading normal lives, cultivating the land, and were also given the liberty to keep their families with them. What was the harm if some forests were cleared? In the south the woods towards Lalkuan were cleared to put up paper mills. They defied the dacoits of Tanda and built housing complexes, colleges and huge farm houses. Man, 'the Predator', even scared away the wild animals of the Kala Dhungi region, keeping some as 'show pieces' for tourists, in the famous 'Corbett National Park', building resorts along the river, after denuding it badly with sand mining year after year! The same has happened to the river Gaula. After years of sand mining, it now becomes extinct within miles of moving downstream out of Haldwani.

Haldwani itself is a prosperous town. Besides the

descendants of the initial few families, who still maintain it as their home base, thousands of people have migrated to the town in search of a lucrative livelihood and rarely have they been disappointed. Happily, joblessness is rare in Haldwani. Even socially, the people are more progressive; I feel the early onset of education, particularly for girls, gives them that edge. Only the green expanse is gone except for my house; it's where I still go, when the affairs of life confound me or tire me, or when I simply wish to be by myself! Luckily, the beautiful boulevard outside my house is still intact, paved now instead of cobbled, but shaded by the same old huge trees. The stream of water flows downstream alongside, rippling in the sun, singing its perennial tune; children and old folks soak in the winter sun and the summer breeze, strolling alongside or sitting beside it; the lazy evenings see lovers chatting away, or dreaming into the setting sun, sitting on its thick stone boundary walls.

Every time, the place re-invents itself and treats me to some new miracle. When Daddy had been in a coma, and was beyond caring for himself, we had dug a pit in a corner of our compound, next to the boundary wall, where we would daily collect his soiled clothes, even pampers and paper napkins and burn them after pouring petrol on them. Then after Daddy left, we covered the pit with earth, and slapped it down with a spade. Two years later, I was visiting Haldwani. One day the servant, who had been with Daddy throughout his last ten years, took me towards the extant pit, and showed me what he had not shown anyone: two beautiful trees bearing custard apples had grown there, in the middle of a patch of grass and weeds. "*Didi,*" he said, "I was waiting for the first fruit of this particular tree to ripen; I wanted to give it only to you to eat, Daddyji has sent it for you!" I looked at the custard apple as if I was looking at a marvel. I patted him and thanked him, and told him I was overwhelmed by his love and loyalty. I recognized the fruit to be the same breed that Bauji had carefully collected from Lucknow and Allahabad. How that particular custard apple came to sprout at exactly this place, with no other plants around, was really a marvel, a miracle created by nature to prove to me something that I had yet not understood in life! That year the tree gave only seven custard apples and I enjoyed the rare sweetness of each; outside cartloads of the fruit were selling all over town, but none had the colour, the texture, the shape or taste of the fruit that grew in my compound. 'Thank you *Bauji*, thank you Daddy, thank you God!' I thought.

And then there is the unique miracle of the Nainital lake that like a pure soul only reflects the calm and serene beauty of the surrounding hills, never any of the unnatural monstrosities created by man. Rowing around the lake, as I do as often as I can, taking the oars from the disbelieving boatman, still lifts me miles above this world, to some divine place, and I feel light in my head and heart! Starting from Mallital boat stand I row down alongside the 'Mall Road' towards Tallital, passing by the ducks basking in the sun. Circumventing the bus stand and the swimming banks, I row to the ancient 'Hanuman' temple, perched on a protruding rock, with its potted wild roses and scores of brass bells, and bow to this sentinel of God, who looks after my favourite town. Then I row upwards along the the Lower Mall, marking every furrow thick with shrubs, every large bare rock lashed by the water, every clump of daisies, every bending deodar, its branches brushing against the waves, like a hoary old lover; crossing the Tibetan Market and the Gurudwara, the Skating Rink and the Band Stand, completing the boat ride at Mallital boat stand, gloriously rejuvenated and ready to take on anything, for at sixty two, if I can row around this huge lake, I am fit and fine, thank God!

Alone at night I sometimes ponder on what life is all about.

Is it a walk into the woods? You enter the well trodden path, walk past the trees, the grass, the twigs and foliage, the tweets and twitters, the scurrying of the squirrels and rustling of bushes, you walk and walk—till you've lost the path, and You and your Jungle are One! Perhaps it is.

Each human being is a Star— one among billions; if you keep looking at one, you'd still lose it among the others—but it has its own special place in the universe!

☺☺☹

Chapter 16

A Reunion

Just as this book was going to the press, the unbelievable happened, and I found my long lost friend after forty eight years.

Komal and I were in high school together, and closer than the closest of friends. We studied together and shared the same ambition of getting into a medical college and becoming good doctors. We were inseparable, spending long afternoons during preparatory leave doing physics, chemistry and physiology, practising hundreds of maths problems, eating fruits and biscuits, often lying in bed sharing fantasies, pondering over our bright future; even sharing our family problems which we normally never did with anyone else. We had similar tastes in food and in clothes, and also in reading. But our focus was on our ambition to study medicine; we would not let anything come in the way, we had decided.

Just a few weeks before the final exams, Komal's father was transferred to Madras, and she too left quickly after the exams. I went away for the vacations till the results were to be announced, for then we would scamper for the college admissions. The day of college admissions was the day that turned my life upside down, shattering my soul. But Komal's letter a few days later told me that she had got admission in Pre Medical College in Madras, and would continue in the same institution till her graduation. Very happy for her, I wrote back to congratulate her, and I don't remember if I told her about my own U-turn. But I did write her another letter when I was engaged, and she replied too. After that I never wrote again. I always planned to. In my mind I would be framing the letters that I would soon write to her, debating how to convey to her the anguish of my broken soul. Weeks ran into months, and months into years. We lost all contact. Later when I got my bearings, I could not find Komal anywhere. My best friend was lost!

Decades went by. I became a mother and a grandmother but I never stopped thinking of Komal. I tried to write a short story about two friends who got separated, but my brain refused to imagine anything, no possibility of what happened could be even fictionalised by me. I had thought if I wrote that story, it would help me deal with my loss, but it did not happen. And life went on.

Then a miracle happened! Early this year we were at a dinner my cousin Honey from Asansol had organised for her friends, when I discovered that the lady I was chatting to was the sister of Komal's father. My head and heart went for a spin. At last I had found Komal, and I had her phone number. I came to know that she lived with her husband in Baltimore in the US, and that her husband was a doctor too, Dr. Dang. It took me some weeks to have this sink in, to be sure, to pick up the phone, and make that call. "Hello," the same sweet voice answered.

" Komal, this is Satvir, we were at St. Teresa's...." and she cut in.

"Satvir! Satvir, wow, I've been trying to locate you forever. I asked everyone I could—anyone related to the motor spare parts business, but couldn't find you." And we were so grateful we now had each other after exactly forty eight years!

Komal called back in two months. She told me she had a private clinic, specializing in Internal Medicine and Geriatrics, and that her husband, a very successful doctor, had just retired. We both shared our desire to meet soon. She said she was busy, so I promised I would fly out in September to meet her. But in September, I mailed her to say I could not travel till January. I also told her that I had never found another friend like her or shared with anyone like I used to share with her.

Two days later I got her mail saying, "I have made an impromptu plan to whiz in and meet you for a day, then fly out to Chennai for an alumni meet , then fly back to Baltimore. See you at the airport." While I was waiting at the airport, she called, "I've just landed. How will we know each other after all these years? I'm wearing black trousers."

And I thought, "Does she think black is so rare that it is enough to identify someone?" I told her, "I'm waiting at the coffee shop, and I'm wearing maroon."

But when she wheeled out her luggage, we didn't need any identification! We hugged, and in that miraculous and magical moment, nearly five decades simply evaporated. We felt as if we had never parted. Komal told my son, "We cannot talk with words today, our emotions will do the talking." And we spent two glorious nights and one day with each other; feeling so much gratitude for the divine power that brought us together. We didn't dwell on the past, just shared our different journeys through life. She told my daughter-in-law, "Satvir will not go in the kitchen today," like only an old friend can. Komal spent the evening meeting and enjoying my children and grand children, hugging them all, while Ricky asked me, "How does one get to make such loving and lasting friends?" She spoke of her three lovely daughters, the youngest a musician like my son Sarabjit and of her three grandchildren, with the fourth on the way. It was wonderful.

Before she left, I said to her, "I am looking forward to both our families getting together and enjoying a great relationship!"

Komal replied sagely, "Let us relish what we are enjoying

today. When more comes, we'll enjoy that too, but if it does not happen, we ought not to be disappointed! One should plan and work towards good things in life, but accept the results happily." Such a simple and profound philosophy.

They say it is foolish to wish for something for too long, particularly foolish to desire something beyond the Mathematical Law of Possibilities. For three fourths of my life I kept wishing to be reunited with Komal, and God finally made it possible; I guess that's why they say that God Loves Foolish People! One should never give up on hope. You never know, you may get to ski on the Swiss Alps for the first time in your life when you're sixty; you may set out on an adventure sailing trip after retiring or you may find the perfect life partner when you're eighty. Perhaps it's always a good idea to dream, wish and believe. For who knows, wishes can always come true.